SURG

Miranda Mason had left England and her
quiet vicarage home to learn more about
life, which was why she had taken the job
of medical officer in a luxury hotel in
Malaysia. And then she fell head over
heels in love with the surgeon Jonathan
Smith—and learned about life rather
faster than she had bargained for!

Lancashire born, Jenny Ashe read English at Birmingham, returning thence with a BA and RA—the latter being rheumatoid arthritis, which after barrels of various pills, and three operations, led to her becoming almost bionic, with two manmade joints. Married to a junior surgeon in Scotland, who was born in Malaysia, she returned to Liverpool with three Scottish children when her husband went into general practice in 1966. She has written non-stop after that—articles, short stories and radio talks. Her novels just had to be set in a medical environment, which she considers compassionate, fascinating and completely rewarding.

Jenny Ashe has written six other Doctor Nurse Romances, the most recent being *Spring and Dr Daley*, *The Pagoda Doctors* and *The Partnership*.

SURGEON IN THE CLOUDS

BY

JENNY ASHE

MILLS & BOON LIMITED
15-16 BROOK'S MEWS
LONDON W1A 1DR

*First published in Great Britain 1987
by Mills & Boon Limited*

© Jenny Ashe 1987

*Australian copyright 1987
Philippine copyright 1987*

ISBN 0 263 75677 7

*Set in Monotype Times 10.3 on 10.8 pt.
03-0387-59211*

*Typeset in Great Britain by
Associated Publishing Services
Printed and bound in Great Britain by
Collins, Glasgow*

CHAPTER ONE

'OH no, Bill, I'm not going up there—not even for you! Let's go home while we're all in one piece.' Sister Miranda Mason was not usually a very timid person. A bit shy, maybe, a bit naïve, but that would pass with experience. She was not timid—but the spectacle before them was both awe-inspiring and very wild. The monsoon was drenching down. The sides of the great craggy mountain, towering above them into threatening mists, were being lashed by a crazed wind, the treetops below them and above them looking as though they would be dragged up by the roots any minute. And the *kabel cerata*, the cable car, on its way down through those thick black clouds, shook like a tiny fragile toy in the hands of a cruelly playful giant.

'Where's that pioneering spirit of yours? You were very brave when we talked this over in a Covent Garden tea-shop,' Bill tried to tease her, but he had to shout above the wind, and his words blew away. And even his expression was less than ebullient. It was only a couple of hours since they had landed at the airport of Shahallah outside Kuala Lumpur in blazing, wonderful heat. England seemed even to Bill suddenly very tiny, to belong to another planet, galaxies away. This was an alien environment.

Miranda shook her head and tried to smooth back her hair, as the wind whipped it across her eyes. 'Oh, Bill, whatever made us think we'd like it here?' The wind howled in baleful answer. The rattle of the cable could be heard through the sheets of rain as the bobbing car descended, looming like a doomed chariot of the gods.

'Money—lovely money.' Bill patted her shoulder, trying to cheer her up. 'You aren't going to let a few raindrops come between us and our fortunes?'

They stood feeling bedraggled in the ramshackle hut.
There was a Chinese family next to them, also waiting for
the *cerata*—mother, father, a little boy and a shrivelled little grandmother. There were two Indian youths calmly
accepting the downpour as routine. There was a uniformed official, not even looking up from his careful paring
of his nails. Miranda stared at them with a feeling of
unreality. If only the taxi from the airport had taken them
all the way up the mountain, to the hotel where they were
to work. But as the road got steeper winding round the
mountain side, and the rain got steadily worse, the driver
had protested. Bill had tried to bribe him with double
pay—the hotel would pay their expenses—but he had had
enough of the conditions. 'You take *kabel cerata*—very
easy, very good. Take you up quick, seven, eight minutes
only.'

Bill protested, hating to drag their suitcases out into the
driving water, but the Malay had stuck to his story. 'Road
become very steep, engine not good. You take *kabel cerata*—see, station there, very easy. I lend my umbrella for
you get to the station.' And he had whipped out an outsize
umbrella, seen them in comparative safety across the car
park which was already a couple of inches deep in monsoon water. The gale did its best to ground them before
they reached the shelter of that corrugated iron roof. At
least he carried their cases for them, making a third trip,
tottering and struggling, buffeted by the wind.

Miranda gave up trying to talk. She just stood, watching the amazing splendour of a Malaysian monsoon
venting its wild energy on the precipices around them. It
was so unreal, so unlike the gentle Berkshire nature that
she knew. Wind and rain had never seeemed so vicious, so
venomous before.

Bill was wrong, though. She hadn't come so far from
home for the money. She had come because she knew she
was naïve, coming from a village vicarage to her nursing

life in London. A job as a medical officer in a luxury hotel she knew would give her more experience of life, more confidence. Even more adventure—which was just what she was getting now. She tried to calm her fear, tell herself she wasn't afraid. The official was not afraid; the Indian boys took it as a normal day. She must put herself in their place. If there really were any danger in taking this cable car, then the staff would surely not run it.

She looked at the others waiting. Oriental impassivity sat on most faces—all except the Chinese grandmother, who was sitting on a bench looking as though she would blow away in the wind, feverishly telling her prayer beads. Miranda's heart went out to the miniature figure as the jade beads tumbled through her thin fingers. She found herself smiling at the wife, who returned the smile but immediately turned away. She must remember that her own brand of open friendliness might not be acceptable here.

The car was almost docked now, the noise of the engine and the rattling cables almost deafening. Everyone, in varying stages of apprehension, moved towards the flimsy gate. Between the car and the gate was a gap. Miranda looked down, then shuddered as she realised just how precariously they seemed to be perched on the face of the mighty cliff. She closed her eyes, clinging on to the rail with white knuckles.

'All right?' Bill was comfortingly close, but he had two cases to struggle with, so could not lend a hand.

'It's a long way down.' She tried to sound offhand.

'Don't look down. Do what I'm doing and take a look at that gorgeous lady conductor.' Bill prided himself on being a connoisseur of beauty, and the Indian woman who stood waiting to unbolt the gate was indeed gorgeous. She had huge black eyes ringed with kohl, glossy hair tied in a loose tail, glittering green pendants in her ears, and a very tight trouser suit. The car docked with a gentle bump. The lovely lady unlocked it, and the passengers disembarked as though getting off the tube at Charing Cross. They made their way nonchalantly to waiting cars, cabs, or the local bus, its wheels half hidden in the flood waters.

Now that the cable machinery had stopped, the wind seemed less noisy. Miranda stood back to let the little Chinese grandmother take the last seat, then she humped her own case over the threshold, and stood on the wooden floor, looking straight out across nothingness, thousands of feet above sea level. Below, interspersed among the tossing trees, were splashes of vivid orange flowers, making the savage scenery lovely in its majesty, set off by the blackness of the clouds above them. She could even see the spiralling road they should have taken like a narrow ribbon between the banks of trees, the cars like toys between waving branches that looked like some mighty ocean.

'Theatrical but enormous.'

Bill arranged his cases out of the way of people's feet. 'What did you say?'

'Dramatic. What a dramatic welcome to Genting!' She tried to be blasée, to keep her voice steady. Would this glamorous conductress actually think it was safe to set off in this wind? She did. A horn hooted somewhere inside the engine room. The ticket seller waved at the conductress from the shelter of his little cubbyhole and she waved back saucily.

Just then one of the Indian boys shouted, 'Someone else coming, *lah*!' It was a couple running the last few feet towards the gate. The conductress unbolted the gate for them, and they entered, thanking her. Bill moved his case again gallantly to make room for the pretty Eurasian woman with a mass of curly black hair. She was wearing a Chinese tunic and trousers in figured satin that showed off a very shapely figure. Good old Bill, he never failed to notice them.

She was out of breath, but the man with her seemed untroubled by their last-minute dash. He was tall, with dark blond hair. Miranda was conscious without looking at him of his height, balanced by broad shoulders, muscular tanned arms in a short-sleeved silk shirt. His long legs were braced apart as the horn honked again, and the car suddenly jerked out into space, out into the sheets of rain.

Miranda closed her eyes again, as the windows and roof were battered by drops loud as gunshots. She was terribly aware of the drop beneath her. In spite of the cool wind, she felt sweat start on her forehead. The sides of the mountains disappeared as they suddenly rose into the very clouds that were sending all the rain. They were lost, depending for their very lives on that one slim cable. . . that very thin, very wobbly cable. . .

'Don't be frightened.' A warm comforting voice. She opened her eyes. It was the tall man. She looked up and saw that he had twinkling blue eyes—keen eyes, the eyes of someone who had to make judgements. He was terribly attractive if not conventionally handsome, and she knew it was his eyes, and the way his humanity and his authority showed in them. He sounded so very kind, so thoughtful to have noticed the panic of a complete stranger. He sounded English. 'This must be your first trip up here,' he said.

Miranda had a strange feeling of safety, that everything was suddenly all right. 'Yes, we're complete beginners. This time yesterday I think I was on another planet!'

The tall man smiled, and she thought he was wonderful to be so kind. He wasn't much over thirty. He looked across at Bill, seeing that they were together. 'It is quite an experience, this little toy, the first couple of times. But I can vouch for its safety. I come up two or three times a year, and it's never let me down yet.'

His deep velvety voice had taken away Miranda's fear. She went to the edge, held the rail, looked down through the patchy clouds without trembling. Ragged scraps of mist curled round the treetops. 'I think it's really quite beautiful—in an eerie, ghostly sort of way,' she said.

The tall man nodded. 'It is beautiful. I'm knocked sideways by the beauty every time—the trees like an angry sea, the Flame of the Forest like real fire, don't you think?' He spoke quietly, looking out at the scenery, not at Miranda. She felt at ease with him. And she understood how he felt. It was magnificent, not frightening at all.

'Flame of the Forest—yes, oh yes! Those flashes of orange—it's as though the jungle is burning.' No longer afraid, eyes shining, she looked around her with a growing confidence. It didn't seem at all strange to be chatting to this tall stranger. She pointed. 'Oh, look—caves! There must be trolls and goblins and dragons in these mountains too.' The cable car swayed in the wind, rattled its way upwards, jolted as it passed one of the concrete pillars that upheld the cable. Miranda smiled in sheer pleasure.

The tall man was suddenly looking at her, not the mountain. She turned, smiled again, in exhilaration at the beauty he had made out of her former fear. His eyes were very blue—clear, intense blue, the colour of a kitten's or the picture of the sky as she had seen it over the white desert in adventure stories. . .

A most unadventurous snort came suddenly. She knew it was from the Eurasian woman, because she had moved noticeably closer to them. 'I hope you remembered the package for the hospital, Jonathan!' She waited, her beautiful face turned up to his.

Jonathan turned towards her with a slow smile, and Miranda stared like a child fascinated by his mobile face—his wholly delightful face. He spoke. 'Mary Ann, would I forget anything of yours?'

Miranda thought how kind he sounded. Was it the voice, so dependable and calm, or the eyes—electric in their vitality? But at that moment even her childlike admiration was distracted—the clouds parted with the touch of a magician's wand. Everyone, even the cool laid-back Indian boys, gasped, shifted in their places as the lovely shaft of golden sunshine sloped down to them as though it came direct from heaven. The wind calmed as it had in the Gospel. For the final few yards of their ascent they rode up a mountainside bathed in light, rocked by nothing fiercer than a baby breeze.

The car rocked a little, juddered and stopped at the station. Mist swirled and parted, and above it, Miranda suddenly saw a city of gleaming white like fairyland or the giant's kingdom at the top of the Beanstalk. The engine gave a last shake as it shut down, and she lost her balance. Jonathan, the kind tall man, caught her in his arms and steadied her, and she found herself looking up into his nice face, smiling a little awkwardly—and then finding she couldn't look away. The blue, the calm yet disturbing blue. . . She smelt his male smell, felt the warmth and roughness of his arms as they held her tightly. For a brief second she had the feeling that he didn't want to let her go. The togetherness of that moment was something she was powerless to end.

And then the press of people getting off, the rush controlled by the pretty conductress. Jonathan and his dark beauty were the first off—as though she had dragged him away, ahead of Miranda and Bill, who had their cases to grapple with. They found they were the last on terra firma, the last to step out on to their first bit of the City in the Sky. Miranda said, 'Well, here we are. I'm so excited! The land over the rainbow.'

Bill was unaccoutably cool. 'Oh, very James Bondish.'

'Don't be grumpy, Bill. Come on, let's explore.'

'Okay, okay. I've got more luggage than you.' Miranda was too preoccupied with looking around her to notice his lack of enthusiasm. She hoisted her shoulder bag on her left arm, and lifted her case with her right. What awaited them? The air was so cool and fresh, totally different from the sweaty plains of the city. It was easy to see why the Malaysians were refreshed in a place like this.

'We're right inside a hotel, aren't we?' she asked.

'It's not ours. We have to find the way out of here, and the Empress should be directly opposite.'

'What a good idea, having the cable car bring the people straight inside.'

'It's carefully worked out, my innocent child. The Casino is in here. Those in a hurry to get rid of their money only have to take the elevator.' Bill nodded towards the sign to the Casino. 'Come on. The way out must be this way.'

Miranda trotted after him, gazing all around her as they walked. 'What a décor! It's like a film set. And look, Bill—what a lot of women are going to the Casino!'

Bill grunted. 'Their husbands are all at work earning the money for them to lose, I expect. Hurry up, Miranda, I'm getting hungry, and I could use a drink.'

'Right, oh leader. It's this way—I saw the arrow.'

They were soon down in the entrance hall, slowly getting used to the sheer size of their surroundings. Outside were still more gleaming white buildings—not fairy palaces at all, but functional holiday flats, with balconies and decorative greenery at every window. The sky was pale blue now, reminding her of home, that small sleepy village half a world away. 'Do you think the Empress will be as grand as this place? I'm going to love it.'

'You'd better. We've got a year to do—no use chickening out.'

Miranda laughed. 'Bill, don't make it sound like a prison sentence! You do like it, don't you?'

'Very much, kid. I can smell the money.' He sounded sophisticated, but she knew he wasn't much older than she was. But he was right. All the guests they met, all the streams of people on the way to the restaurants and the Casino were well-dressed and well-bejewelled. And the cars outside were long, sleek and expensive.

She said primly, 'You're mercenary.'

'You aren't turning the money down.'

'I came for the—excitement, Bill.'

He managed a smile. 'Let's go and find it, then.'

The great white face of the Empress was almost opposite. It rose, the décor imitation Chinese of the great Dynasties. The road was lined with blossom trees, and the grass verges were green, luxuriant and peppered with flowers. They crossed the road and walked wonderingly into the high mirrored foyer of the Empress Hotel. Immediately a tall Sikh in a gold turban came to meet them. 'You are expected, Mr Thorne, Miss Mason. Welcome and salaam.'

They put down their cases. 'Thanks very much.' Bill shook hands with the Sikh. 'Do you like it here?'

The Indian nodded his magnificent head, and the jewels in his turban glittered. 'Is very nice, Thorne Sahib. Holiday places always nice—everyone happy, relaxing, eating and drinking and enjoying.' He winked. 'Everybody generous, Sahib.'

'Roger and out,' Bill waved, and bent to pick up his case. But the elegant doorman held out a hand.

'Luggage will be taken to your rooms, sahib. You sit in Suzy's bar—there, across hall. I see if Mr Heng is back yet.'

Suzy was a very pretty Chinese girl in a tight cheongsam, her hair in an elaborate chignon, long waterfalls of pearls hanging daintily from her little ears. Her bar was nicely situated, with a good view of the foyer—excellent for people who were waiting for dates. She came forward as Bill smiled and introduced them both. 'Bill and Miranda.' Miranda could see Bill's mood undergoing a quick about-face at the loveliness and the attentiveness of the mistress of the bar. 'We're more than delighted to make your acquaintance.'

She laughed that high-pitched tinkling laugh that sounded like Chinese music. 'And now I make you more than delighted by offering you welcome drink on house.' She placed them at a small table where they could look around the great expanse of hall and grand staircases.

Miranda saw that all the notices were in Malay first, then English, Chinese and Tamil. She was reading the one entitled, 'Casino Rules,' aloud to Bill.

'You can't gamble at all if you're a Muslim. You must wear a tie and shoes, not sandals. You must wear a long-sleeved shirt—batik, Bill—have you got a batik shirt?'

''Course not, woman. You buy them here, not in Marks and Spencers.'

Suzy brought them tall drinks, pale frothy liquid over crushed ice. There were lots of bubbles at the brim, and a slice of pineapple on the edge. Whatever it was, it tasted heavenly. Miranda realised how thirsty she was. The last refreshment they had had was at the airport, a million miles away, it seemed now.

'Miss Mason? Mr Thorne?'

A wiry little Chinese in an immaculate three-piece suit was holding out his hand, and Bill jumped up at once. 'Good day, Mr Heng.'

Miranda shook hands too. 'It was wonderful of you to have us here.'

'Any friend of Kim is my friend. My son is not an idiot. He has often written about you all, and what a happy group you had at the Poly—is that where you all were?'

'The North London Poly. Most of us. Miranda was working at the Charing Cross Hospital, but she was friendly with Fiona. . .' Bill stopped, hand to mouth.

Heng smiled. 'I know Kim was—er—going out—with Fiona. But no longer. Now that he works for me in Kuala Lumpur, he takes life more seriously.'

'I hope we get a chance to meet up,' said Bill.

'I will not work you too hard, Bill. You are familiar with the work of a hotel manager?'

'Oh yes—worked at the Hilton for my business training.'

'Good. I will enjoy having you here to help. Your office is next to mine. But we will talk of work tomorrow. You have come a long way, and need some time to find your way about.'

Miranda's turn. Kim's father turned and smiled at her. His teeth, like his cuffs and his watch, gleamed like gold. 'You two are—going out together?'

Miranda shook her head, wishing she didn't blush so easily. 'No, not at all, we're only friends. But my father was glad that someone was coming with me whom he knew. It's the furthest I've ever been from home, and I'm an only child, you see.'

'You have good qualifications. You know you will be in sole charge of the first aid room? Our other nurse has decided to go and work at the Genting Hotel.'

'I won't mind that,' said Miranda. 'I've done plenty of casualty.'

'Very good indeed. Well, I'll leave you to settle in. I see that Suzy has welcomed you with our customary secret formula.' Beaming at his wit, Mr Heng nodded and left them.

'Well, all right so far, Miranda?' queried Bill.

'Fine. But this Empress special is making my head swim. I bet there's vodka in it.'

'You haven't eaten since lunch, no wonder it's gone to your head. Let's go and have an unashamedly luxurious shower, then decide which of the seven restaurants we want to eat in tonight. Here's your key. We're in the staff wing. Kim said even the littlest chambermaids have wonderful accommodation, so ours should be something pretty nice.'

Miranda craned her neck as they went up the gracious staircase. Surely it wasn't real gold, all that glitter on the lamps and the cornices? She had noticed that all the glasses in Suzy's were real crystal—or looked it. Fresh flowers abounded, chrysanthemums and orchids, palm leaves and white frangipani like fragrant stars.

Their rooms were adjoining. Miranda unlocked her door and entered, delighting in the thickness of the carpet.

Then she saw Bill grinning at her through the common door, and ran over to close it. 'Nothing personal, Bill. You're a good enough friend to be shut out without being offended, I know.' They had been part of the same group for a long time, but only since they began to plan this trip had they become friends. They enjoyed each other's company, but there was no question of it going any further than that. Miranda in fact was awkward with men, never having known anyone of the opposite sex of her own age at school or even when she did her training.

And then there had been Trevor. . . Again she blushed at the thought. A rather spotty houseman at Charing Cross, trying to look big, impress the girls. Miranda forced herself to look out of the window at the excess of flowering cherry trees. She didn't want memories of Trevor to come between her and her new and exciting employment.

The mist was closing in again around the tall white buildings, as night fell. Still a little fuddled by the drink, she gazed down at the taxis below, at the elegant gowns and tuxedos beginning to arrive for an evening at the Empress. She felt a shiver go up and down her spine at being part of such a new and different scenario. She looked across at the Genting Hotel, where so short a time ago the cable car had delivered them. It had been thrilling, riding up the mountain. And Jonathan, the tall, sweet-natured man. . . Genting was not such a big place; she might see him again. He might even need medical attention.

She smiled as she unbuttoned her dress, unpacked some of her things, pulled a thick white towel from the rail, and began to run the shower. Her own private and very swish bathroom—not much like Charing Cross. And she knew that it was the presence in this small plateau of land up above the clouds of a certain man called Jonathan that really lent the last sparkle to her excitement. She recalled the strength of his arms, rough with little brown hairs. . . the silk shirt, smooth to her cheek as he held her, stopped her from falling. . .

There was a tap on the door, and Bill came in. She hadn't bolted the adjoining door properly. 'Aren't you ready yet?' he queried.

Miranda peeped out of the shower. He was resplendent in a dinner suit. He wasn't bad looking; his eyes were grey-ish, and they didn't crinkle at the corners like Jonathan's did, making her spine tingle. 'Don't wait,' she told him. 'I'll meet you in Suzy's.'

'I'll wait. I promised the Reverend Mr Mason.'

'Daddy won't mind if you're a minute or two before me. Give you time to chat up the glamorous Suzy too!'

Miranda had gone back into the shower. She heard him call, 'If you're a minute more than five, I'll have died of starvation!' She smiled as she towelled herself with vigour. Reminding him of Suzy was the best way of getting him to go.

She chose a silky dress that hadn't suffered too much in packing. It was dark green, with long sleeves, and she decided it suited her dark brown hair and eyes. She knew she was no beauty, but she couldn't be bothered with looking at that oh, so familiar face long enough to make up her eyes or cheeks. And she too was hungry.

There was a rather tall thin man waiting for the lift. He wore jeans, which surprised her, as most people were dressing for dinner. He had a gingerish beard and fluffy hair, and freckles across his nose—and a friendly smile, as he realised that Miranda was eyeing him. 'Evenin', Prin-cess. You're new around these parts.' He was American, obviously. A real Southern cowboy?

Miranda lowered her eyes modestly. 'I'm the new med-ical officer.'

'Gee!' It was an expression of great delight. He held out his hand. 'I'm Jake Dempsey—the tall one in the singin' group. We used to be four, but two of 'em got bored, so now there's only Maidie and me.'

'I'm Miranda,' she smiled. His handshake was firm and honest. 'Where do you sing? We'll come and listen.'

The lift swished up, and they entered, still chatting. 'Orchid Room—that's the best. But Maidie and me'll be slung out when the great Sheikh himself arrives next week. Back to the Blue Lagoon, we'll be. You don't look impressed, Princess. You've heard of Zendik, haven't you?'

'I think so. He's Australian, isn't he?'

'Princess, sound more enthusiastic, willya? He's top of the bill—the greatest thing in South-East Asia. All the girls are crazy about him.' They stepped out of the lift together. 'Now there's a guy to melt you, you little English ice-box.'

Miranda laughed. 'I'm not impressionable, Jake. I think I'd rather hear you and your Maidie.'

'Great, I'm not complainin'.' He turned towards Suzy's. 'Buy y'a drink, Princess?' he looked back at her. 'Say, there's a guy lookin' at you in a funny way.'

She grinned. 'It's only Bill, the new assistant manager. We're together. Except—we're not, if you see. . .'

'I know exactly.' Jake strode across. 'Hi, Bill.'

'Hi. Join us?' Bill was taken at once with Jake's easy friendliness.

'Hell no, man. Your first night—drinks on me. Maidie won't be long—at least, she might be, but we won't wait.' The big American could be forceful. 'Suzy, honey chile, four Singapore slings—big ones.'

Miranda opened her mouth to protest, but the slings had already been placed on a corner table—probably Jake and Maidie always sat there. They were surrounded by potted palms, yet could see all the ritzy comings and goings in the foyer. While they sipped their drinks, Jake gave them the names of all the staff they should know, making them laugh with his casual but observant remarks about them. Miranda had thrown back her head, her laughter encouraged by the drinks, at Jake's description of Maidie's ability to wiggle her hips—when a figure came in that made her heart lurch. She sat back quickly, hiding behind the waving palms. It was indeed Jonathan. He wore a white tuxedo. His lovely companion was in shimmering silver, slit to the thigh. What a stunning couple!

Jake had seen Miranda's face change. He leaned across the table, and said in his slow Southern drawl, 'I thought you said you weren't the impressionable type, honey?' He was looking at her with a lazy teasing smile.

'You don't miss much, Jake Dempsey!' she joked, to hide her sheer physical reaction, the heightened colour, the disturbance in her breathing. One man having that effect? Yet it had just happened. Miranda realised that she had a lot to learn about herself. Trying to keep her voice casual, she said, 'Incidentally, Mr Knowall, who is that?'

'One of our regulars. Mr Smith to you.'

'Smith?' Miranda forgot her discomfiture in a hearty laugh. 'He's incognito, is he?'

'No, Princess. Jonathan Devereux-Smith is a cardiac surgeon—the Devereux Klinik in KL. Nice guy—calls himself Smith because he's no side.' Jake leaned forward. 'Real nice guy. Comes up here three, four times a year to unwind. Plays a little blackjack, drinks some wine, brings a beautiful dame—never the same one. Knows how to relax, does Mr Smith.' Jake winked as he drained his glass.

'Jonathan Devereux-Smith. What a mouthful!'

'Don't call him that, if you get to know him. I told you, no side to him. He likes to be plain Mr Smith.'

Bill was slightly scornful. 'You're behind the times, Jake. She already did get to know him—threw herself into his arms on the cable car. They made quite a spectacle of themselves. His girl-friend was furious!' Bill too had drunk more than usual on an empty stomach. Miranda wished he hadn't said that.

'The car jerked,' she said hastily.

'Don't give me that! You gazed up at that bloke as if there was no tomorrow.'

Jake was grinning. 'Not impressionable?' But his voice was gentle. He knew when to stop teasing. 'When Zendik arrives no other men will get a look in anyway.'

Bill obviously knew more about the famous Zendik than Miranda did. He raised his eyes heavenwards, 'That Indian pop singer? I know him—descends on the females with all the delicacy of a nuclear explosion!' He smiled at Jake. 'Not my type. But I didn't know he was due here. I've always wanted to see for myself if he really is as good as they say.'

Jake shrugged. 'Personality, I guess.' He turned round. 'I say, Maidie's here just in time. Let's eat.' Maidie Schu-maker had arrived like a fairy on a sunbeam, tiny, blonde and curvy with a face as sweet as sugar—standing by the lanky Jake she looked as though she would blow away. She turned to Bill and Miranda with a breathy excuse for being late, and Bill was instantly besotted.

'Gee, you folks are so wonderful to wait for me. I'm starving—the smell of garlic and prawns is driving me crazy!' She led the way to the Orchid Room, and Miranda had to admit to herself that Jake was right about the wig-gle. Maidie wore a white mini-skirt fringed with silver. Her hair was fluffed out like candy floss, and she wore three-inch diamanté earrings. Dressed for the stage, all right. Bill's eyes never left the cowboy hat that hung down her back on a sequinned string, that bobbed about as she walked.

By the time they had eaten the first course—the prawns that Maidie craved—the four of them felt as though they had been friends for ever. Miranda had some trouble with her chopsticks, but the others and the waiters were helpful and easy. The lavishness of her surroundings thrilled her every time she looked up from her plate. She was just beginning to feel limp, the effects of jet-lag and all the excitement.

Mr Heng had stopped at their table and snapped his fin-gers for a free bottle of champagne. He was resplendent in a shiny dinner suit and red carnation. 'My compli-ments. I look forward to an enjoyable year.' The wine arrived at once in a gleaming silver pail, and the head waiter bowed and offered Miranda an orchid spray for her dress, before opening the bottle. She felt her spirits bubbling with the wine.

Jake refused a second glass. 'Time for my intro.' He went out of the room, reappearing with beard combed, a broad cowboy belt slung round his hips, and a rather shabby guitar. He strolled past them, wandering up to the stage as though by accident. Idly he began to strum a few chords. There was no formal announcement, but as he strummed the chatter in the restaurant died down. Gently, as though to himself, Jake began to sing.

'Maidie, he's brilliant,' whispered Miranda. Jake's voice was like melting honey. He sang of simple things, of farms, fields of corn, sweet wild fruits and sweet country girls. He sang convincingly of lazy sunshine and the simple life. Miranda almost saw the golden corn waving behind him.

'He's okay.' Maidie had pride for him in her voice. 'Time to liven things up around here. Hold on to your hats!' She winked at Bill, and skipped up quickly to join her partner. There were cheers just for her pert appearance. She did her famous wiggle before setting herself jauntily in front of Jake, and putting her hands on her shapely hips. Then from that dainty figure came the heartiest female voice they had ever heard. There was laughter and much applause for her gutsy style. Bill and Miranda just kept on clapping, won over by the talent of their new friends.

They did a couple of conventional duets then, country music that had feet tapping with them. Then Maidie came forward and took the spotlight. The lights dimmed. She smiled, sweetly as a child, the epitome of innocence, and sang: 'I'm a little prairie flower,
    Growing wilder every hour,
    Nobody cares to cultivate me
    So I'm as wild as wild can be.'
Maidie Shumaker turned that simple ditty into a blockbuster. She knew how to sell a song, and the audience rose

to her. She smiled and bowed, and smiled again, kissing her hands to them. In the midst of the applause, a portly Chinese man stepped forward and handed her a spray of orchids, calling wildly for more.

Suddenly he stumbled and fell hard. Miranda's professional eye spotted at once that it was no ordinary loss of balance, and she ran forward. The man lay clutching his throat. His lips were blue. The woman with him screamed. Miranda bent down, loosened his collar and flung his tie away. 'I'm a nurse. It's his heart—ring for a stretcher.' She knew the Genting Hospital was only minutes away along the road, but minutes were now vital.

Bill knelt by her. 'Can I do anything?'

'Just get them to hurry.' There was a laboured gasp from the recumbent figure. She turned him on his back and felt his pulse, but she couldn't detect any. 'On no, hang on there,' she murmured, putting her hands firmly on his sternum, and beginning to thump as hard as she could. 'Don't stop, don't stop,' she prayed silently.

Suddenly someone else was kneeling. 'You a nurse?'

'Yes. There's no pulse.'

'Okay. I'm a doctor. I'll massage while you mouth-to-mouth, okay?' Whoever it was knew what he was doing. Miranda pulled her hair back from her face, bent and forced the man's lips apart, breathing gulps of air into the lungs. He was totally unconscious now. The thumping beside her seemed to go on for ages. She breathd and gasped for air, then breathed again into his mouth. Then she saw his eyelids flicker weakly, and knew that they had won. The stranger stopped massaging, and mopped his forehead with a handkerchief as the cry came from the door to make way for the stretcher. 'I'll go with him.' He got to his feet, and held out a hand to help Miranda up. 'That was great work, Nurse.'

They stood for a moment, gazing into each other's eyes. That blue, that perfect blue. Time stood still. Then he murmured again, 'Thanks, great work,' and turned to take the patient's wrist as he was carried out of the hushed and silent restaurant. They heard the medical team in the distance, and then silence, before the scraping of chairs as diners began to sit down again.

CHAPTER TWO

MIRANDA sat down, feeling numb. It was perfectly natural for a doctor to go to the aid of a sick man, just as it was normal for Miranda to go. There was nothing romantic like fate drawing them together—merely their medical training. Yet as she had stared up at that elegant figure in a white tuxedo, she thought she could hear angel choirs, and the music of *Kismet* swelling around them both, the forces of something powerful she had never felt before.

Maidie broke the spell with her plaintive Southern drawl, as though it was all her fault. 'It was just the same in Baltimore!' And Jake patted her hand, comforting her. It wasn't her fault that she was pretty. The big blue eyes were round with shock.

'He'll be okay, Maidie.' Miranda tried to reassure her too. 'The heartbeat had come back quite strongly. Mr Smith must be very strong.'

'I'm proud of you, Miranda.' Bill was the first to recover. 'That's showing them, saving a life on your first day here!'

'I'm tired. I think I'll turn in.' She refused company and walked up the gilded staircase rather than take the lift, to give her jumbled thoughts time to settle down, her emotions a few moments to try to recognise what had happened. Weary as she was, the excitement of the day made her toss and turn for a while in the luxurious king-sized bed. She kept on hearing him say, 'Great work', in that admiring way. And then she saw the beautiful face of his companion just behind him.

She woke after a deep and untroubled sleep, feeling wonderful. There was a delicious fragrance in the room, one that made her want to get up. It was fresh tea. A maid was drawing back the high curtains, and a beam of bright sunlight dappled her bed. A tray with a china cup and saucer lay beside her. 'You like tea each morning?' The maid was cheerful, Chinese and petite.

'I'm not a guest. I work here,' Miranda explained.

The maid laughed. 'I bring tea to all the people. No trouble bring to you and Mr Bill.'

'Fair enough. Thanks very much, that's lovely.' If they were to be spoiled by the management, they would just have to get used to it. She drank her tea, admiring the delicate china. Then she showered, and dressed in her new dark blue uniform dress, fastened on the silver-buckled belt. She decided against wearing a cap—that was official enough. She brushed her hair back. She felt a bit guilty leaving it loose.

There was a tap on the door, and a breakfast tray was brought in—hot croissants, butter, small bananas, slices of papaya and pineapple, a silver pot of coffee. Miranda sighed with pleasure. Then she noticed that the knob of the door to Bill's room was being rattled, and she unlocked it. They breakfasted together, equally delighted about the start to the day.

'You look every inch the tycoon today, Bill,' she told him. In his new tropical suit and dark tie, he looked older and more mature. She told him so.

'Fancy you noticing! I thought you had eyes only for Jonathan.'

'Don't tease. I hardly noticed him.' There was no point in telling Bill how she felt; he would only make fun of her. 'You are a smart and good-looking man, and I'm proud to be with you.'

'You look pretty efficient yourself. Here's to our year at Genting.' They drank the last of the coffee, and went down together.

The medical room was vacant. Miranda's name had been put up outside on a plastic plate—Sister Miranda Mason, Medical Officer. It looked businesslike. She went in and sat down. The desk was shiny, there was her own phone, the cupboards appeared to have all the equipment she might need. The maid came with coffee at eleven. She leaned back in her comfortable chair, and thought how much her hard-working friends at Charing Cross would envy her this place. All she needed now was customers.

By the time Bill looked in at lunchtime, she had seen one man with a hangover, and one with a bruised knee where he had fallen down some steps. She was wondering if it would look bad if she fell asleep in between patients, when Bill came in. 'Come on, Miranda. You don't have to stay here all the time, you know. You look as though you've taken root! Just make sure that Reception know where you are.'

'Oh, I see.' She felt embarrassed. 'Am I too enthusiastic?'

'No, love. You'll soon find out what the job involves. Now come and have lunch.'

Just then they heard a child crying, and Miranda smiled. 'You go, Bill. This sounds like a job for me.'

'Okay, if you don't mind.'

Miranda saw him out and admitted a worried-looking mother with a sweet but sad little boy. 'What's his name?' she asked.

'Ho Kai. He say pain is in neck, this side.'

She felt sorry for the little chap, tears oozing from his black eyes. But she felt pretty sure she knew what the trouble was. 'It's an earache sort of cry. Let's see.' The ear was inflamed inside, causing pain all round the affected area. 'Is he allergic to penicillin?'

'I do not think.'

'Okay, fine, Ho Kai. Soon be well again. Hold him still, please.' She gave him an injection of penicillin, then gave the mother a bottle to give him four times a day. 'He should feel better quite soon,' she told her.

She put away the injection things. When she turned round, there was another patient standing in the middle of the room, his face contorted with pain. 'I trap my fingers in door.'

Miranda smiled. 'Sit down. We'll soon do something about that.' Were all her patients going to come when she wanted her lunch? She used an antiseptic on the red raw gashes in three fingers, and put a comforting dressing round them, using plenty of cotton wool. The man's face looked a lot less anguished as he thanked her. She put the bandages away, and then almost sighed as she heard the door open again. Not more emergencies!

'Miranda?'

She knew whose voice it was without turning round from the cupboard. 'That's my name.'

'I thought it must be. It says so outside.' Jonathan Smith was strolling towards her, looking at ease and very handsome in white jeans and short-sleeved tee-shirt. 'You don't mind, do you? I've come to heap praise upon you.'

'I don't mind. But I am just on my way out.'

'That's why I came at this time. May I buy you lunch?' He was so very calm. Miranda tried to stop her heart jumping around inside her ribcage. He was so very—experienced. Yes, that was the word. And she was suddenly frightened. She had hoped to see him again, but his self-confidence was so opposite to her own lack of sophistication that she wanted desperately to refuse.

Forcing her voice to stay level, sound cool, she said, 'It isn't necessary.'

'I know that. But it was the only excuse I could think of for getting to know you better.'

Very conscious of her unmade-up face, her severe uniform, she said, 'Oh!'

He smiled, reading her thoughts, a warm smile. Almost in a whisper he said, 'Miranda, please have lunch with me?'

She was unaccountably hoarse as she said, 'I'll have to let Reception know where I am.' She coughed and felt awkward.

'Sure. Tell them Sam's.'

'Where's that?'

'In the basement. They know.'

'Of course.' Miranda rang the desk and told them. She knew Jonathan was looking at her as she made the call. From being an attractive man, he was suddenly something of a threat, and she wished she didn't have to spend a whole lunchtime chatting to him. She turned slowly. 'I'm ready,' she told him.

They walked easily along the corridor, Jonathan fitting his long strides with her shorter ones. 'You look much older in uniform, Miranda,' he remarked.

'That's a good thing anyway,' she smiled.

'Yes. Today you look almost fifteen.'

She looked up at him. It was a joke, but even as she smiled, it made her feel even more raw and inexperienced. 'Almost ten years out.'

'You aren't twenty-five.'

'No, twenty-four.' Well, she was allowed to add on an extra year, surely. And she knew how young she was, for all of those twenty-three years.

'I'm thirty-four.' He didn't seem bothered. 'Age isn't really important, you know. Some people are born middle-aged.' She could think of nothing to say. But she knew what she was thinking—that a successful man as good-looking as Jonathan Smith ought to be settled down with a nice wife and family. But Miranda didn't have the confidence to be so personal on their first meeting.

Sam's place was in the basement, and dark. There was a candle on each table. It was meant to look secretive and special—she noticed at once that the tables were only for two—a place for lovers, obviously. She felt even more confused, and slightly breathless with apprehension. A pianist played smoochy music—even in the middle of the day. Miranda wasn't used to such degenerate surroundings, but she couldn't help a little giggle of excitement. Jonathan was quick to agree. 'Yes, you could say it was a bit over the top, I know. But he does a marvellous pizza.

I love Chinese food, but now and again Sam's pizza calls out to me. Do you mind?'

'Oh no.' Miranda sat down, smoothing her uniform nervously over her knees. She was glad of the dark—those piercing eyes couldn't look across and read her thoughts.

'Penny for your thoughts,' he said.

'Well, your—er—the girl with you—she doesn't mind if you lunch with someone else?'

'She has no idea. She doesn't each lunch—and anyway, when I left her she was in the sauna.'

Miranda giggled again. At Jonathan's request to know what was funny, she admitted, 'It just sounds so—decadent, I suppose.'

He laughed heartily. 'Isn't it just?' He didn't mind her being personal, then. His voice changed. 'I have to admit that I did want to get to know you, since I saw you on the cable car. I felt I had to look after you—and then I saw there was a young man already lucky enough to have that job.'

That was good—he saw that she wasn't alone and defenceless, then. She said, 'That poor man last night—it wasn't a very auspicious way to meet. How is he?'

'Mr Suk is pretty well. He did have an infarction, but he's strong. He'll pull through. He's in the hospital, if you want to go over and see for yourself.'

'Thanks. I will, later.'

Sam brought them dry Martinis, and Jonathan ordered pizzas. Miranda began to relax a little. This man wasn't the ogre she had imagined, after her honour. He was just nice to talk to. 'Mr Suk was lucky to have such a high-ranking heart man around when he had his attack,' she remarked.

'So you know my line of work? Yes, I think he's a candidate for coronary bypass. But I'm not exactly touting for customers at the moment. I've got more on my plate than I'd like. Luckily I've got a superb partner, and we relieve each other when the pressure mounts.'

'Pressure is one of the factors, of course. You take time off to keep your own arteries in shape?' He nodded. Miranda went on, suddenly finding she had no fear of Jonathan Smith, 'Don't you think a prevention unit would be a good idea? Regular checks, ECGs and BPs? Maybe some physio advice?'

'You're right—it's needed. I suppose we're just too busy at Devereux to give it any thought.' Jonathan was enjoying his pizza as they talked, but he suddenly said, 'I'm thoughtless—I should have let you try something local. The food is so familiar to me. But you ought to have tried *nasi limak*—something Malay and delicious.'

'I've lots of time for that.' Miranda's eyes were used to the dimness now, and she was beginning to enjoy lunching with the nicest man in Genting. She stole little looks at him as he ate, admiring the look of casual confidence, the man of the world. His hair was naturally wavy, and she watched the way it curled over his tanned forehead, round his ears, that strong neck. . .

He caught her looking, and she was glad of the dark as she felt her cheeks grow warm. 'One year? It will soon pass.'

'How long will you be staying?'

'For ever, Miranda, for ever.' He deliberately made it dramatic. 'You must know it's like breaking into Fort Knox to get back into the magic circle of British cardiac surgery once you've left all your contacts. No, I have a good life here.' Was that a tiny sigh? 'I'll be here till my number is up, I dare say. And what pleasanter place to be? You'll find out, Miranda. KL isn't what it was in the days of the British, but it's a place and a half when you get to know it.'

'We have a friend there,' she told him. 'It will be nice to get to know it.'

'Give me a buzz if you've time. If you like, I'll show you round the Devereux.'

'Thank you.' Miranda was interested. She went on to question him about his work, about how many government places he had, as opposed to private, and how many staff. It was luxury compared with what she knew in London. On the other hand, the stresses in a surgeon's life were all too familiar to her.

The conversation was natural and fascinating. Neither Miranda nor the handsome Jonathan seemed to want it to stop. When she looked at her watch, and said she must get back, he came with her, chatting all the way. It was only when she saw Bill in the foyer that Miranda felt a warning signal somewhere in the back of her brain. She knew what it said: For goodness' sake be careful! You're a complete beginner in the art of life. If you don't take care, you're going to be badly hurt.

She turned to Jonathan. Not wanting the embarrassment of introducing him to Bill, she excused herself rapidly. 'It was very kind. I did enjoy our talk.' And at double speed, she was in her office before Jonathan had moved away.

Bill came in, puzzled. 'Hey, what was all that?' he wanted to know.

'Nothing. We had lunch.'

'Well, great. Why the drama?'

Miranda went over to the window and stared out at the pretty cherry blossom, the fountain in front of the hotel, spouting water like tears. 'I'm scared,' she confessed. 'I just had a lovely time. But, Bill, I'm so ignorant. I don't know if he's really nice, or just shooting a line—he's had so many women, he must be good at chatting them up. How do I know I might not have ended up in bed with him? I don't, Bill. I was so much under his spell that I might have, so as not to look naïve. . .'

'Bad as that, was it?'

'It wasn't bad, it was lovely. That's my problem.' She still stared out, unseeing. 'He would be wonderful, I know that. But then I'd be the one left in the sauna while he went off after the next fancy.'

'The sauna?' Bill was out of his depth.

'Where he left the glamorous female he came up with. He laughed about it too!'

'I don't know what to say,' muttered Bill.

'Good. I'm frightened of men who always come up with the right remark. You're nice, Bill. I like you.'

'Thanks.' He smiled. It wasn't the sort of smile that sent needles of desire to all available parts of her body, like Jonathan Smith's. It was a safe smile, steady, predictable. Good old Bill! Miranda sighed deeply, breathing in the freshness of the garden. She said calmly, 'It's over now.' It was a statement.

'Sorry you came?'

'Not a bit. I've just learned a lesson: never play with fire.'

'Miranda, you're too sensible to get burned. I'm sure of that.'

'Or lucky.' She tried not to think of what might have happened if Jonathan Smith had happened to be the amorous type. Would she have had the strength of mind to refuse him, when physically she knew she responded in every gear?

Bill went back to his office, while Miranda sat at her desk and wished she had a job that kept her busy. This was a joke of a job. Four patients a day wasn't her idea of work. Her thoughts were back with Jonathan, writing a speech in which she told him to stay with his floozies and leave her alone. Then suddenly Maidie Schumaker was standing in front of her, very real and very frightened, eyes huge with fear, gripping her wrist from which red blood was dripping on to the carpet. 'I cut myself,' she said faintly.

Miranda got her to the sink. 'I can see that, Maidie. Come and drip in here while I decide what to do.' Miranda might get hot under the collar with men, but medical emergencies brought out the best in her. 'What did you do that with?'

'Nail scissors. I fell on them.' The pretty American looked calmer now.

'That wasn't very bright.' Miranda mopped the clotted blood away to assess the depth of the wound.

'I know. I guess I won't walk about when I'm doing my nails any more.' The colour was coming back into the round, childlike face. 'It could have been serious, couldn't it?'

'Very serious.' Fortunately no major vessels were involved, but the cut was still deep. 'I'll have to put a couple of stitches in, Maidie, or you won't be able to go on tonight.'

'Oh, okay.' Resigned, Maidie held out her arm on to the sterile cloth Miranda placed on the couch.

'Maidie, think of something beautiful. Look out of the window.'

'I guess I'll think of chocolate cream gateau. I'll never in my life ever be able to have any—I gain weight too fast.' Maidie looked away as Miranda, with a little smile at Maidie's idea of something beautiful, quickly poured antiseptic into a bowl. The edges of the wound were clean, so it was a straightforward task to fix them together. But it took five stitches. As she knotted the last with nimble fingers, she praised her patient for keeping so still.

'I know you don't want bandages. Just let me put a thick one on for now. I'll change it for a small dressing just for your performance.'

There was a charge at her door, as of a wounded rhinoceros. It was Jake. 'Waal, what do I think? Blood on the floor, and no sign of Maidie?'

The patient said sharply, 'I hope you called the maid to clean it up.'

'The maid? Honey, I called the whole damn hotel to find you.' He sat down at Miranda's insistence, and she saw his hands were shaking.

'Tranquilliser, Jake?' she offered.

'Thanks, Princess. You're a pal and a half. Was she a pain in the ass?'

Miranda gave him a Valium. 'She was a model patient,' she assured him.

Jake swallowed his pill. 'Hell, she's changed a lot.'

Miranda looked at them both. They made no protestations of affection, but it was clear enough how Jake felt. 'Take her up,' she instructed. 'Make her sleep, Jake.'

He obeyed. With his long arm loosely around little Maidie's shoulders, he edged her out of the room. 'Come on, honey, grab some sleep like the lady says.' Miranda looked after them. In a short time she had become fond of the two Americans. And with the work she was doing so very scanty, life would be rather dull without the friendship of Jake and Maidie.

The medical room seemed very quiet. She could hear happy voices outside on the tennis courts. She sighed. Maybe when she got to know more people it would be more interesting. Bill was lucky, keeping busy.

Jake stuck his head around the door. 'She's sleeping, ma'am. How about we grab us both some coffee?'

'Thanks, Jake.' Anything to pass the time. 'There isn't much to do around here, is there?'

They sat in the Japanese Lounge drinking coffee. Someone came in and strummed at the grand piano in the corner. He looked like the pianist from Sam's, now at a loose end like Miranda. She admitted to Jake, 'I'm not used to doing nothing for a living.'

'Life is easy here,' he admitted. 'Stop me if I'm out of line, but I can't quite fix you and that Bill.'

Miranda looked across at the length of him, stretched out way past the chair that part of him was sitting in. 'We aren't lovers,' she explained, 'just friends in the same lodgings in London. Mr Heng's son was one too. Quite a nice crowd, we had.'

'You want it that way?'

'Sure. Why?'

'You ain't in love?'

She imitated his accent. 'We sure ain't.' She tried to explain how Kim had painted a rosy picture of life in Malaysia, and how she and Bill were both in the sort of job where a year off doesn't affect the promotion prospects.

The pianist began to play some Chopin, and it sounded odd in this Oriental palace. Time dragged. Jake asked, 'How's the heart attack feller?'

'Mr Suk? He's doing all right. I was going to visit him later.' Miranda sat up. 'Which is the hospital? I'll go now. Want to come?'

'No way. Hospitals smell I can't take.' But Jake pointed out the white green-roofed building not far along the cherry-blossom-borderedroad. Miranda let the desk know where she would be, and went out into the calm sweet-smelling afternoon.

The hospital doors were green slatted, and she pushed them open tentatively. The darkness inside made her blink at first, then slowly she made out pale blue carpets, creamy painted walls with flower prints at intervals. Fresh hibiscus and bird-of-paradise flowers in brass pots stood in every corner. There was a large wooden desk in the middle of the entrance hall, but nobody behind it. The atmosphere was hushed and peaceful—not a bit like the hospitals Miranda was used to.

A young Chinese nurse in crisp uniform came along the corridor, her feet making no noise on the thick carpet. 'Can I help you? I'm Sister Tan.'

'I'm Miranda Mason—Sister at the Empress.'

The other girl's face brightened. 'You are the one who saved Mr Suk. Come in, Sister Mason. You wish to visit him?'

'If it's allowed.'

'Oh yes. He is much better now.'

'That's good. He was lucky Mr Smith was there,' Miranda remarked.

'Very lucky.' Sister Tan pointed. 'This way. His heart had stopped, I believe?' Miranda nodded, reliving those frantic few moments. The other girl asked, 'You like to look around the hospital?'

'Sure, if you aren't busy.' Needless question; there was an air of complete calm. 'I wish I was working in a hospital. The hotel work is really kid stuff.'

Sister Tan laughed. 'We would be glad of help with night duty. I'll tell Dr Moon, if you are interested.'

'That's great.' They walked around the ground floor, Sister Tan explaining each department. Miranda asked, 'Are you from Genting?'

'From Kuala Lumpur. And you?'

'London.'

'Ah, I have always dreamed of going there one day.' Nurse Tan became confidential. Her name was Cherry, and she had an open friendly manner that appealed to Miranda. They chatted happily as they made a tour of the entire building. 'This is ICU. Mr Suk is in this room.' They went in quietly, but the businessman was lying quite at ease, still connected to the monitoring instruments, but holding a *Straits Times* before him, reading the financial section. 'Mr Suk, you have permission to read?' But the nurse's voice was gentle as she introduced Miranda. 'You did not see her face last night, Mr Suk.'

His face broke into a large grin and he held out a hand to her. 'I am fine. Mr Smith tell me that he started my heart after it stop. But he also say that you put the air in my chest, make me breathe again. I am fortunate indeed. Both very kind, very good peoples.'

Miranda smiled. 'Glad to help.'

Mr Suk wanted to talk. 'He tell me also no more to eat the fatty things, always to exercise.' He grinned again, showing a large selection of teeth. 'Then I do not again become so excited at pretty American girl with the curvy legs!'

Sister Tan became alarmed at their hearty laughter, even though she couldn't help joining in. 'Enough talk for one visit, Mr Suk,' she said severely.

On the way back to the door, Cherry said, 'Mr Smith is a wonderful man, so kind and friendly. You would not think he is such a famous surgeon. He acts just like an ordinary man.'

Miranda kept quiet, feeling a sudden wobble in her knees at the talk of the man she had shared lunch with. 'Yes, I noticed.' She shut her lips tightly together, as adjectives like devastating, overwhelming and attractive came unbidden to her tongue.

'He is very friendly with Dr Moon.' Cherry was just beginning to tell Miranda the names of the staff at the hospital, when a junior came running.

'There is an emergency, Sister—a baby, not breathing. Dr Moon has been called.'

Cherry went at once, inviting Miranda to join them. The junior ran in front, opening the door to Casualty for them.

Cherry came in, while Miranda stood in the doorway and gasped. Hastily she covered her mouth to stop distracting the two figures bent over the child. One was the lovely Eurasian woman she had first seen on the cable car. She was wearing a white coat, bending over the figure of Jonathan Smith, brushing his cheek with her long hair. He was sitting, a baby on his knee, listening to its chest with a stethoscope.

He didn't notice the newcomers. He was murmuring to the baby. 'You can do it, sweetheart. Don't give up, my love. Come on, little one, keep trying.' He waited for a moment, then looked up at his lovely companion. 'She's going to make it, Mary Ann. The tachycardia has settled. Lucky you had the right drugs down here.'

'Lucky for me. I don't want a brat die on me—bad for my reputation.'

Jonathan Smith looked away, his face expressionless. He listened to the tiny heart again, then lifted the child, wrapped the shawl around her, and laid her against his shoulder, where she looked even tinier against those rippling muscles.

Miranda felt a lump in her throat. How very tenderly he held the little Malay baby! How soft and caring his voice, a contrast with the young woman's harsh declaration about 'the brat'. The more Miranda saw of this man, the more she admired him. She had been reluctant to accept his invitation to lunch, but now all she could do was pray that he would ask her again. She felt a twinge of envy of the tiny baby, who nestled so trustingly against his shoulder, felt the touch of his lips on her downy little cheek. . .

Sister Tan said, 'Thank goodness! You don't need us, then, Doctor.'

The Eurasian woman looked across, her pretty face hard. 'No.'

Jonathan looked up then, and his face changed as he recognised Miranda. 'I say, we have reinforcements, Mary Ann. This is the girl I told you about—Sister Miranda from the Express. I hope you have permission to play truant, Miranda.'

'I—' Miranda swallowed, and tried again, her mouth dry. 'I—came to see Mr Suk. When there was an emergency, Cherry thought I might be useful.'

'Very thoughtful, Cherry.' Jonathan smiled. 'Thank God all is well.' He turned to his Eurasian beauty. 'This is Dr Moon, Miranda—Mary Ann Moon.' He left the two women eyeing each other, as he crossed the room and laid the baby gently in a cot.

CHAPTER THREE

AFTER a pause, Mary Ann Moon smiled at Miranda. It was a lovely smile, showing a perfect set of white teeth in a gentle heart-shaped face. But it was empty of feeling. 'How nice to meet you.' The dark sloe eyes belied the words.

'How do you do.'

Cherry said, 'Sister Mason doesn't mind doing odd nights for us, Doctor.'

'I'll be glad to take you up on that, Sister.'

Miranda explained, 'There really isn't a lot to do at the Empress.'

The lovely woman nodded. 'And you have Sister da Costa too, have you not?'

'No, I'm alone.'

Cherry said, 'Da Costa was transferred to the Genting at her own request.' She chuckled. 'She was a dragon of a woman! It's nice to have someone young and with a quiet voice.'

Mary Ann Moon nodded again. 'We weren't the best of friends.'

Miranda didn't want to be friends either, but she wanted to keep the peace between them. 'Well, I'm no dragon. Just let me know if you need me.' She turned, feeling that the interview was now over.

Jonathan Smith turned round. He looked younger, his hair dishevelled where the baby had grabbed it and held on. The white tee-shirt showed off his tanned arms, and those blue eyes pierced through the afternoon, until Miranda thought she could never look away. 'What did you think of Mr Suk, Miranda?'

'Incredibly well for an infarct.'

'Terrific constitution. And a great sense of humour. He'll pull through.'

He seemed quite content to chat. It was Dr Moon who looked ostentatiously at her watch. 'Jonny, we did promise the Count we'd meet him for squash. Do you want to call it off?' Her tone was impatient. Naturally enough, thought Miranda. If she had a man like that, she'd want him to herself too.

Jonathan said, 'Oh, lord, I forgot! No, Mary Ann, don't call it off, for goodness' sake. I want my revenge. Fancy letting a man of fifty beat me!'

His energy and good humour were infectious. It was hard to resist him. It was even harder to be the first to turn away. So Miranda just stood, and basked in the golden presence of Jonathan Smith. Cherry went over to the cot. 'Shall I let the mother come in now?' she asked.

'Oh yes, Cherry.' He looked across, where the baby slept on her side, breathing normally. 'All is well at the moment. But I think she should stay in overnight.' Cherry went to the door and brought in a young Malay woman with frightened dark almond eyes. Jonathan was sympathetic. 'She's fine now, but I—Dr Moon—would like to monitor her for twenty-four hours. Do you want to stay with her?' He pointed to a low bed in the corner.

'Yes, please.' The woman gazed up at him, and then tears welled as she looked across at the cot. 'She will live?'

'Definitely. What's her name?'

'Jasmine.'

'Well, my dear, you can take her home with you tomorrow. Dr Moon will see her first thing and give you the all-clear.' He looked down at the baby. 'I'll miss her—she's beautiful.'

Mary Ann appeared to lose patience. 'Show Mrs Kalih the hospitality room, Cherry.' She turned away, showing that the whole business was over. At the door she turned.

'I can call you, Miranda, if we need a night Sister?'

'Sure. Just let me know in good time.'

'I will. The pay is good.' She fluttered her eyelashes at Jonathan Smith, as though distinguishing them from the paid underlings like Cherry and Miranda.

'The pay is immaterial,' Miranda said shortly.

Mary Ann wasn't listening, looking up and laughing at something she said to Jonathan. She clearly put her own love-life above anything else—she was even unable to treat Mrs Kalih with any sympathy because she had arrived with poor little Jasmine just when they had arranged to play squash. Miranda murmured her thanks to Cherry, and hurried outside for some fresh air. Somehow the mental picture of Jonathan with Mary Ann was distasteful, offensive.

When she returned to her room and rang the desk, there had been no patients for her. It was an empty sort of job, and she was glad she had taken the trouble to look for extra employment at the hospital, Mary Ann or no Mary Ann. It would fill the time. And Cherry Tan was nice. They could become friends.

It was almost five. Miranda tidied her already tidy desk, and left the room. Jake Dempsey appeared suddenly, his tall frame clothed in white. 'Play tennis with me, Miranda. No one else will.' He carried two rackets, and the shorts made him look even taller than the jeans.

Her eyes brightened. 'I'd love that—if you aren't too good.' She had the sudden wicked thought that she could work off her aggression by pretending the ball was Mary Ann. . .

'Nah. Lousy.' But when Miranda returned to the courts in her white dress, she quailed. Jake was knocking against a wall, fringed with blossom trees. And his power was formidable.

'Jake, you're a professional! I insist that you use your left hand.'

He grinned his lazy grin. 'Okay, if you say so, Princess. But I'm left-handed.'

'Oh, you know what I mean. Give me a chance.'

'No way.' He sat down on the bench before they started to play, and hauled up a long leg to fasten the shoelaces tighter. 'See how you let me put you off? Even before we started you've lost. That's no way to play life, kid. You have to look as though you mean to give the other guy hell. Don't admit you have any weaknesses. Think of your strengths, and go out there to give all you've got.'

Miranda nodded. He was right. And he put it so well. 'You're a pal, Jake. But tell me—are you really good?'

He stood up and swung his racket fiercely. 'I'm great. How about you?'

She paused, knowing he wanted to hear if she had learned her lesson. 'I can beat you, Jake Dempsey.'

'Right on. Try me, then.' They knocked a few balls about. She soon found that in spite of his power, he was lazy and would not run for shots which she would. 'Okay, kid, let's try a set.'

She had got into the habit of copying his accent. 'Okay, coach, sock it to me!'

Miranda didn't win the set. But, puffed and happily pink, she got two games, and Jake had to try harder than he had first thought to beat her. She trotted in alongside her lanky friend. She had completely forgotten her annoyance with Mary Ann. The sun was low in the sky, colouring the pale turquoise with pink and yellow behind the pink blossom trees. She looked up and grinned at Jake. 'Thanks, pardner—for the advice as well as the game.'

'Shucks, you'd soon have worked that out for yourself.' He put an arm round her shoulders for a second. 'See you in Suzy's.'

'Right.' It was nice. Already her mood had lightened. She had made another friend, and Jake was a treasure. The Empress wasn't such a bad place. There was plenty of time. And it was good to be the accepted companions of the singing stars. Miranda ran up the stairs rather than wait for the lift.

She showered vigorously, and chose a pretty blue dress with a full skirt to go down to dinner. She didn't wait for Bill. They had already started going their separate ways, and enjoying it. That was the best thing.

Maidie was last down to Suzy's, and she walked with less than her usual bounce. She wore a gingham outfit, and her candyfloss hair was tied in two bunches. 'I changed the dressing myself. Didn't need to bother you, Miranda.' She held out her cut wrist. She had covered the wound with a flesh-coloured plaster. 'Is that okay?'

Bill hadn't been told of Maidie's accident, and he looked full of concern. 'You shouldn't sing tonight. Jake doesn't mind, do you, Jake? You look very pale. Jake, tell her she's better taking it easy.'

Jake's smile was slow and delightfully crooked, Miranda thought. 'Billy boy, I never tell Maidie what to do. But if I were her, I'd give the gig a miss, especially after losing all that blood.'

Bill's face looked even more perturbed. 'You lost blood? In that case—'

Maidie was petulant. 'Quiet, you-all! I had a long sleep this afternoon and I feel fine.' She inspected the hand. 'It doesn't show much, does it?' It was Bill who took the little hand in his, and inspected it closely. Maidie seemed pleased at the attention, and Miranda saw that Jake was pretending not to notice.

It was taken for granted that the four of them share the same table for dinner. Miranda, who was in good spirits now, drew Jake out to talk about his career as a star. He amused them with stories of his singing life, from Florida to Los Angeles, from Las Vegas to Baltimore, where he had met Maidie and they had decided to team up with another couple. By the time Jake went up to do his act, all panic about Maidie had ebbed away, and tempers were cheerful. Again Miranda listened spellbound to Jake's lazy, arm voice, while Bill eyed Maidie with more than average attention.

Miranda was just beginning to feel it was time to go to bed, when the uniformed pageboy bowed politely. 'Telephone for you, Miss Mason. Shall I bring it to the table?'

'No, I'll come.'

'Is hospital, miss. Can you spare them a minute?'

'Of course.' Miranda didn't mind tonight. She had ended the day calmly, taking note of Jake's affection for Maidie, Maidie's indifference to him and growing interest in Bill. It was a touching little charade, highlighted by Jake spotlighted, singing 'Secret Love' in his lovely sentimental voice.

She tapped Bill's arm, bringing his attention back from Maidie with difficulty. 'I'm going to the hospital, in case you wondered where I was.' He nodded, and turned again to the stage, to Maidie's pert figure swinging her hips, blatantly twinkling at Bill as she sang the duet with Jake. Miranda slipped away.

The street was quiet, almost deserted. On both sides were the lighted windows of the great hotels, full of people enjoying themselves. There was distant music from several sources. At the Empress pool there was laughter and splashing from those swimming by floodlights and moonlight. Miranda crossed the road, the fragrance of the flowers at night reminding her a little of home.

Cherry Tan came to meet her as she opened the slatted doors. 'Thank you for coming. Nurse Lam has been on duty all day, and there's been an emergency appendicectomy. He has a temperature, and needs hourly monitoring. Think you can manage?'

'No problem. I can sleep in the morning. They don't usually need me until lunch time down there.' Miranda looked down at her full-skirted dress. 'I say, you wouldn't have a spare overall, would you? Peacock blue is hardly a restful nursing colour!'

Cherry smiled, and found her a clean white overall. They made their way along the shadowy corridors. The postoperative patient lay still on his back, fast asleep, his breath coming in long gasps. Nurse Lam was standing by him, and was clearly relieved to see Miranda. 'It is very good of you,' she whispered.

'I'm glad to help. How is he?'

'Temperature is raised—thirty-eight.' She showed the chart. 'But I think he has started to respond to the antibiotics.'

'And I'm to check him hourly?' Miranda settled herself in the small room adjoining the ward, where she could see the patient but not disturb him with her reading lamp. The armchair was very comfortable.

'Please. I will be back at seven.'

'Fine.' She made sure she had the phone number of the surgeon, whose room was in the next block, just in case of trouble. But the patient looked peaceful enough. There was a pile of magazines in the corner, but Miranda had decided that now was a good time to start her diary of life in Genting. She had bought a notebook specially, and so far nothing had been written except a little note entered on the flight to Kuala Lumpur: 'Have decided I like being waited on.' She smiled, and entered today's date.

It was quite easy to remember all they had done since that fateful ride in the *kabel cerata*. It was harder to describe it without revealing the effect Jonathan Smith had made on her. She mentioned his blue eyes—but not the heart-stopping way they crinkled at the corners just before he smiled. No mention of the velvet voice. No word of his charm and friendliness. No allusion to the magnetism, the fresh male smell of him, the roughness of his arms when they caught and steadied her. . .

She heard a sound at the door. Her cheeks warmed at being caught even thinking the things she was. She looked up to see a thinnish Indian in a crumpled shirt and loosened tie. 'I'm Mr Ghosh,' he told her.

'I'm Sister Miranda Mason.' Mr Ghosh was the surgeon who had operated on the patient in the next room. He smiled, showing even white teeth. 'The patient hasn't stirred, sir.'

'Shall we just take a last look at his temperature? He's young and tough. I'm not expecting any complications, but one likes to be certain.'

The patient mumbled in his sleep as Miranda slipped the thermometer under his arm. He opened one eye when she withdrew it, but immediately went back to sleep as she was checking it. 'Thirty-seven point five,' she read.

'On the way down—good. Call me if you have any worries. Well, goodnight, Sister Mason. I hope you have a quiet night.'

Miranda went back to her diary, recording the events, but avoiding the emotions. She heard a noise upstairs—footsteps, someone coming home from an evening out. She recorded the sentence, 'Did a night's duty at Genting Hospital,' then closed the book. So far, it had been rather more interesting than she realised. The job itself was boring, but she had saved a life, met Jake and Maidie. . . and got to know Mr Devereux-Smith. . . She sat for a moment, the words of Jake's song lingering in her mind—'So I told a friendly star. . .' Miranda looked out of the window. It was a clear sky, freckled with stars. There was a white, perfectly round moon gazing back at her with a great calm and serenity.

'Is it you, Miranda?'

A male voice whispering. At first she thought it was her own imagination, then she turned, alert but not afraid of that comforting voice. There was a shadowy outline in the doorway. Had Mr Ghosh come back? 'Yes, it is. Who's that?'

He moved forward, so that his face was visible in a shaft of moonlight. It was Jonathan.

Miranda froze, suddenly realising that it must have been his footsteps she had heard, upstairs in Mary Ann's room. After an amorous evening with her, was he now coming down for another conquest? All the assurance she was beginning to learn from Jake, and from life, flew out of the window, and she was tongue-tied, shaking, unsure how she felt. She stiffened as he took another step towards her. He seemed to sense her reaction, and stopped several feet away. 'How is your patient?' he asked.

'Doing fine. Temperature coming down slowly.' Her voice was a trifle husky, and she cleared her throat, and waited for him to leave. He went into the ward and took the man's pulse, nodding approvingly.

'It's nice of you to give them a hand,' he remarked.

'I enjoy it.'

'You aren't tired?'

'I can sleep in the morning. The Empress isn't very busy.' She had begun to relax a little, in spite of her earlier apprehension. The man was so genuinely kind and thoughtful. It was nice of him to stop and chat.

'I say, how about me making you a cup of coffee?' he suggested. 'You won't find it easy to stay awake all night.'

'No, thank you, don't trouble. I'll make one when I feel weariness coming on.'

'I'd love one,' he admitted.

He wasn't exactly pleading, but it seemed churlish to refuse when he put it like that. He was really so very charming—and clearly found it easy to get his own way. 'All right, I'll put the kettle on,' said Miranda.

'No, no, you sit there and watch your patient. I'll put the kettle on.' Jonathan waited until she sat down again before coming in and filling the kettle from the sink in the corner. 'Anyway, you don't know where the decent stuff is.'

And you do, of course. You who charm the birds from the trees, and the medical staff into your arms. . . you who must spend many a happy evening here. Miranda knew it was all true, but she was powerless to protect herself from the magic. There was no escaping it.

And as they sat together in the silver moonlight, sipped good coffee, swapped stories about their training in KL and London—she knew she was totally happy, totally at ease, totally content to let this night go on for ever.

'And now I'd better go and get some sleep before a hard day's gambling tomorrow.' Jonathan looked across at her, to see if she took him seriously. 'You won't be afraid of the trolls and goblins by yourself?'

She smiled back. 'No, they're only down in the mountain caverns. They can't harm us up here on the plateau.'

'You're right, Miranda. This is Shangri-La. Nothing can hurt us here.' His voice was so tender at that moment, his eyes so expressive. She almost begged him not to go just yet. He came towards her, stood for a moment looking down at her. She wondered if he was thinking of kissing her. But he just leaned across to pick up the coffee cup, and took them both to the corner to rinse. Then he sighed. 'Well, goodnight, Miranda.'

He was gone before she could think of something to say. Tongue-tied again. Why did it always happen when she wanted to be witty and amusing? She sat still, trying to analyse what had happened to make this one of the loveliest nights of her life. Nothing had happened. Jonathan Smith had sat beside her, chatting and drinking coffee. He had been close, but had made no attempt to touch her. Yet she had been enveloped by his personality, with warmth and pleasure at being near him, important to him. She shook her head hopelessly. What chance had anyone against such a man? He attacked even by staying away, charmed by just being himself.

She thought back to what he had told her of his work. It was almost worth having a heart operation to know you were being cared for by such a man, exuding confidence and reliability. She looked at the empty space in the doorway so recently occupied by his broad shoulders, his tall desirable body. It looked very empty indeed now.

She couldn't have slept even if she wanted to. Her thoughts were electrified and wouldn't stop spinning around in her head. She shook herself mentally, stood up and smoothed down the borrowed uniform. One more temperature and BP to do before Nurse Lam came back on duty. How the night had passed! She could already see the glow on the eastern horizon, heralding the sunrise. The birds had begun to chirrup in the trees, to squabble and flutter. She picked up the sphyg and went in to her patient.

He moaned a little, opened his eyes, and said huskily, 'I'm most terribly thirsty.'

He was English. 'Would you like a cup of tea?' asked Miranda.

'Very much. Are you Florence Nightingale? What angel wakes me from my flowery bed? Shakespeare.'

'I know. I'm Miranda Mason. Are you an actor?'

'Agent, love. Nigel Croft to you.' He stirred and winced. 'God, these stitches are tight!'

'You sound better anyway.' She shook down the thermometer. Yes, his temperature was normal. 'You're allowed an injection for the pain.'

'Nothing that a good cuppa won't cure.'

'Coming up.' She went over to the kettle. As it hissed and spat towards the boil, Miranda fingered the cups that had so recently been washed by a certain tall, charming cardiac surgeon. . . She lifted them gently, wondering which one he had used, which one had touched his sensitive mouth. His enfolding presence flooded over her again, and she felt sexually stirred even at the simple thought of Jonathan's body standing on that spot.

'How long have you lived here, Florence Nightingale Mason?' The voice from the ward brought her back to earth.

'This is my first night.' She smiled through the door. 'They don't often have emergencies, it seems. Tea is just brewing.'

'I've just come too. Started with the belly-ache while driving up. Rotten bad luck, I suppose, but at least I'll be better when Zendik arrives.'

'You've come up to see him too? He must be good.'

'I'm here to try and persuade him to do a British tour, sell a few records.'

Miranda helped Nigel Croft to raise himself on his pillows, and gave him his tea. As he sipped it as though it were nectar of the gods, she said, 'This Zendik fellow sounds terribly special. No, don't try to talk. Concentrate on your tea.'

By the time Miranda went up to her room that morning, jet lag and the exhausting emotion of the night combined to send her fast asleep in seconds. She went down to the medical room at noon, feeling slightly guilty, even though the desk knew where she was. There had been no patients. She sighed a little. It was a good job for someone who wanted to have a holiday, but she didn't like the long dull intervals.

She welcomed Maidie with delight when she walked into the medical room. 'Hi. No more cuts?'

'No, Miranda. I've come to tell you that the three of us are going swimming before lunch. Go and get your costume.'

'You ought not to get that hand wet,' warned Miranda.

'Okay, Mein Führer,' Maidie's Southern drawl made even the simplest statement pretty, 'I'll sit on the edge and look allurin'.'

'That's allowed,' grinned Miranda. 'Won't be long.'

She came down minutes later, wearing a cotton shift over her bikini. She stopped at the desk. 'You have a patient,' the receptionist told her.

'I might have known!' Pulling the shift decently over her suit, Miranda ran along to the medical room, where a white-faced Australian girl sat glumly by the desk.

'Mother made me come,' she explained. 'It's my period pains, Sister.'

'I think we can help you there.' Miranda chatted with her for a few minutes, gave her lots of sympathy and some analgesics. After she had gone, she waited for a little while, but no one else arrived, so Miranda phoned through to say she would be at the pool and then at Suzy's for lunch. As she walked along the corridor towards the heated pool, she frowned slightly. No one could have imagined that a cushy job like this was a pain in the neck. It was just boring. She had been so busy in London, life had been a constant challenge. It didn't need her high level of training to hand out pills for tummy-aches. The job could almost be done by a slot machine. The thought cheered her, and she was smiling as she joined the others at the poolside.

Bill was clearly finding his job highly enjoyable. He was supporting Maidie, who was swimming with her legs while keeping her hands out of the water. This could have been by chance, but the spare hand was naturally clinging fairly tightly round Bill's neck, caressing it gently, as he carried her along with a blissful expression.

Jake had launched himself into the deep end, and was covering the pool incredibly quickly and apparently effortlessly. Miranda joined him, doing two lengths before retiring from the race, unable to keep up. Jake completed another two lugubrious lengths without looking at anyone, then hauled his long body from the water at Miranda's side and ordered two gin slings from a passing waiter.

They sat in friendly silence for a while, sipping their drinks. She looked at him sideways. 'Don't think too hard, Jake. Don't you realise how thrilled I am to be sitting next to a real celebrity?'

He looked at her and gave his first lazy smile of the morning. 'How old is your Bill? Do you think he knows he's fooling around with someone old enough to be his ma?'

'Does it matter?'

Jake sipped his sling, biting with a melancholy slurp the slice of pineapple on the edge of the glass. 'I guess not.'

'How old are you, for goodness' sake?' she asked. 'You sound a hundred today!'

'Thirty-four. Maidie's thirty-six.'

'She looks like a girl. How does she manage it? How do you both manage to look like the kids next door?'

He grinned at her again. 'How old is Bill?'

'Twenty-five. But does it matter? Some people are born middle-aged.' Miranda knew who had said that to her, but tried to keep Jonathan from her thoughts. She said quietly, 'Jake, don't be gloomy. If you aren't good company, you'll drive Maidie even further away from you.'

'I guess you're right,' he sighed.

'Anything else wrong?'

'Perceptive lady. Zendik is coming, that's what. He walks into the limelight like it belongs only to him. Hell, I don't hate the guy, he just messes everything up around the place.'

Miranda patted his sturdy thigh with a slapping sound. 'I promise not to be dazzled by the famous Zendik. I dislike him already, Jake. You know I'm your greatest fan. I know what really good singing is.'

'Princess.' Jake tried not to look pleased. 'Come on, race you, I'll give you a length start.'

She pushed him in, laughing. Just at that moment the phone rang, and an attendant said there was someone in the medical room. Miranda shouted to Bill that she was wanted, and ran off to rub herself down and change quickly.

The medical room was full of people. 'I'm Sister Mason,' she told them all.

'Sister, my brother has the very bad pain in the stomach. He will not go to the hospital.'

The patient himself was a Chinese in his thirties. The crowd around him consisted of both parents, a sister and a cousin. The mother begged, 'Please help him, Sister.'

Miranda sensed something abnormal in the great family shared emotions. 'I think I'd better examine him on the couch alone. Would you wait outside for a few moments?'

They refused to leave him. They clung around their relative as though Miranda had some awful designs on him. It was strange. She tried to deal with them tactfully. 'Perhaps if you help him on to the couch, and then stand back a little while I check him.'

While they did so, she asked a few questions about the family, and it soon appeared that he was the youngest in a family that had lost two sons at birth. He had been delicate as a baby. It seemed to Miranda that he had enjoyed being the baby so much that he had continued doing it into middle life. He was probably pretending he had a pain, to get attention. All the same, she examined him very carefully, to give herself no room for mis-diagnosis.

She listened very carefully to his heart. It sounded strong and regular. There were no sounds in his lungs to show any signs of infection. His nervous system reacted normally to all the reflex tests. His face was a healthy colour, and showed no sign of anaemia.

'And now, can you show me the exact site of your pain?' The family had stayed back, but as Miranda started to prod the patient's abdomen, they crept back one by one, until she was surrounded again as she gently explored the tummy. She realised that it was good to let them hang around. They chatted to him in Cantonese, and she was able to press all areas of the abdomen while his attention was wandering. She noticed that he would clench his teeth, and stiffen his muscles at one spot—but then when she touched that spot when he was chatting, there was no guarding at all. She smiled to herself. They obviously thought that he should have some treatment. They were showing their devotion as a family by making a fuss.

Miranda went to the cupboard and took out a mild antacid for mild indigestion. She stuck on an official label, which said 'The Mixture. Take as directed.' She would not spoil the family's holiday fun by spoiling it with a few home truths about themselves—though back in London she would have referred him to a psychiatrist. 'Give him this exactly half an hour after every meal for the next three days. Don't miss a dose, will you?'

She could tell by the eagerness with which the mother grasped the bottle that they were now happy, having showed how much they loved their son. 'Thank you, Sister. *Terimakasih*. He will recover?'

'I don't think he'll need operation,' replied Miranda, keeping her face straight. 'Goodbye, Mr Kai. Take things easy for a few days.'

She smiled as they left, all the family insisting on shaking hands with her. 'You have been very good.'

By now she had missed lunch. Bill was already back at his desk. She told him about her latest patient, then wandered along to the poolside bar for a sandwich and a rest. She had enjoyed that swim with Jake, and the chat. He was such a nice man. Now there were only children in the pool, chasing one another like baby dolphins, and screaming with happy laughter.

The cafeteria manager came over as she sat at one of the pool tables. 'Miranda, it is the doctor from the hospital.'

Miranda went to the phone on the counter. 'Miranda Mason.'

'Dr Moon here. I believe you saw a Mr Kai this morning?'

'Mr Kai and his family?'

'Yes, he has some relations with him. What did you prescribe?'

'Milk of magnesia. There was nothing wrong with him.'

'Really?' There was something wrong. Mary Ann sounded smug.

'I examined him thoroughly,' Miranda assured her.

'Mmm. Of course you aren't a doctor, so I suppose it isn't your fault. He was brought in just now with paralysis of the left side.' There was almost triumph in her voice. 'He has had a stroke. You slipped up in your diagnosis.'

'His CNS was perfect.' Could Kai really have had a stroke?

'All I can say is that you missed the obvious.' Mary Ann paused, but Miranda said nothing. 'And the family are aware of your negligence. I have admitted the patient. The family think they ought to sue you for malpractice.'

CHAPTER FOUR

MIRANDA'S conscience was clear. She didn't take any notice of Mary Ann and her silly threats. She had done her work conscientiously, as she always did. She had seen patients like Mr Kai before—attention-seekers. She was convinced that the reason for Mary Anne's call was to dicomfit her. Why she disliked her there was no knowing, yet the combination of threat and gloating at her mistake—if mistake it was—could not be ignored. Much as she disliked the whole idea, Miranda knew she must go across and see that patient again. She had to be sure that Mary Ann Moon was speaking the truth, and that Mr Kai really did have a left hemiparesis.

She paused for a moment in the luxurious entrance hall, outside the offices of Mr Heng and of Bill Thorne. Ought she to warn them that a complaint might be made? She felt even more fed-up with the job by now. Most of the time it was nothing, and then suddenly a serious accusation. She decided not to tell anyone. If the charge were negligence, then she was not guilty. She had spent nearly an hour with that man, missing her lunch. That could be verified, so there was no problem. She walked on past the doors.

The blossom trees and the taxi-drivers lazed together in the afternoon warmth. It was a nice place. Miranda stopped at the hospital doors. It too had been a nice place last night—last night when Jonathan Smith had joined her in a moonlit silver paradise. Now it lowered over her, its curving roof seeming to cage a dragon—the dragon of professional disapproval—the dragon in the deceptively lovely shape of Mary Ann Moon, waiting with sheathed claws to destroy her peace of mind.

She straightened her shoulders and went in coolly. 'Hello, Cherry. Where's the new patient, Mr Kai?' she asked.

'Nunber seven.' Cherry looked down again quickly at the list she was checking. Miranda turned away with no further conversation. Moon must have told Cherry already that Miranda had been negligent. How could she believe her so readily?

She paused as she saw the relatives in a bunch outside the door of number seven. But she remembered Jake's advice about never showing fear, and marched on past them, and into the small room where Dr Moon stood chatting to Nurse Lam at the foot of the bed where Mr Kai now lay. A junior doctor came in, a young Chinese in horn-rimmed spectacles. He joined the group by the bed. Mary Ann looked up from the chart she was studying. 'Oh, it's you, Sister Mason.'

The three white-coated figures stared at her as though she had suddenly descended from another planet. Miranda was no coward, but she was unnerved by the three alien stares. Trying to keep her voice steady, she asked, 'How is the patient?'

'Complete paralysis of the left side. He's sleeping now.' Mary Ann might be beautiful, but she seemed to take pleasure in being unpleasant.

'May I see him?'

'I think his family will prefer not. You have done enough damage for one day.'

'I examined him,' protested Miranda. 'There was no abnormality of his circulation or nervous system.'

'He saw you with stomach pains?'

'That's right. But no history of bowel disturbance.'

'Well, a nurse could hardly test for bowel ischaemia,' Mary Ann said dismissively.

Miranda fumed. There was no point in staying here. But she said in as icy a voice as she could, 'All I can say is that it came on extremely suddenly.'

The junior spoke then. 'Suddenly, perhaps. But the family were already certain that something was wrong, or they would not have consulted you, Sister Mason.' Miranda looked back into his impassive face. So the hospital were already convinced then, already against her. She had little hope of a fair hearing now. She looked down at the still form of Mr Kai. Malingerer he surely was, but while there was an element of doubt, she could only feel pity for him and his over-protective family. She went out, past the waiting relatives, who murmured something in a low voice as she passed.

There was no one about that she knew in the Empress. She went to the medical room, and sat for a while at her desk, wondering if she could really stand a whole year of this type of existence. The maid tapped at the door with Chinese tea, but Miranda refused it, and went through to Suzy's bar. There was hardly anyone there at this time of day. Suzy was sitting reading a magazine, a little transistor radio on close to her ear. She seemed to have no trouble enjoying this type of life, with its long spells of idleness.

She looked up and smiled as Miranda came to the bar and sat on a tall stool. 'You like a drink, or you just got nothing to do?'

Feeling reckless, Miranda said, I'll have a drink, please, Suzy. Will you squeeze an orange, and put a measure of vodka in?'

Suzy raised her eyebrows. 'Gosh, Miranda, you too young to drown your sorrows, isn't it? Is it Bill? I notice that he have not time for you and me now that Maidie Schumaker come along.'

Miranda had to laugh at that. 'Maidie is lovely, a real character. But I don't somehow think that twosome will last very long.' She took the tall glass from Suzy.

'Don't be sure. Maidie is wild about that English accent, thinks it's great to be treated with such good manners.'

'I see. That's the attraction.' She didn't mind at all.
Bill was not likely to come to Malaysia again in the near
future. It was nice if he got from this year what so far
Miranda hadn't—fun and an interesting job. 'Suzy, do
you mean to say you fancy him too?' she smiled.

Suzy laughed that tinkling laugh. 'Miranda, you are
teasing me!'

At that moment a very handsome young Indian
entered the foyer. Miranda was looking in that direction, and she spotted him at once—so smart, so self-
confident, in a light grey three-piece suit, a gold watch
and bracelet on his wrist. His glossy black hair was
expensively styled. He looked first at Mr Heng's door,
then at Suzy. Suzy followed Miranda's gaze, and gasped,
'Hassan!' Then she ran towards him, her slim young legs
very obvious through the long slits in her cheongsam.
Her hair flew out behind her. 'Hassan, you are here!'

Miranda watched, trying not to make it obvious. The
two young people stood close together, almost but not
quite touching. She loved the way the races and colours
mixed in Genting, just as it ought to be everywhere. After
an exchange of greetings, Hassan turned, and the two of
them came towards the bar. Suzy's dark eyes shone. Bill
Thorne didn't rate too high on the Suzy scale, then. Her
body was taut and vital suddenly. She caught at Miranda's arm. 'This is Hassan. He is the manager of the
famous Zendik. He come in advance, to make sure the
preparations are all complete.'

Hassan turned his black eyes under severe black brows
towards Miranda. They looked very all-seeing, very
critical. But his smile cleaved the olive skin with dazzling
whiteness. He held out his hand, British style. 'You are
the Sister here? Miranda, if you don't mind I call you
that, you are a hundred times more attractive than Sister
da Costa—even though she is of my race I can say that.'

'Thank you, Hassan. I've never met the lady.'

He smiled again. 'Steer clear if you value your hearing!' He looked at Miranda's empty glass. 'You will join me?'

Suzy had already anticipated him. 'Vodka and orange for Miranda, and an Empress special on the house.'

'And you, sweet. Take something.' Hassan's way of speaking was gentle towards Suzy. Miranda pretended not to notice.

Hassan was then giving Miranda a very good look, up and down. She wasn't sure whether to be offended or not. But he merely said, again gently, 'There is nothing quite so comforting as an English nurse. Their only fault is that they are sometimes a little too proper. But that only adds to the attractiveness—at least to me.' He lifted his glass to her. Miranda smiled. He was charming—but harmless. She raised her glass to him and drank.

Mr Heng appeared, having seen Hassan from a distance. He beamed as he recognised him. 'You flatter us by coming early. Unless you do not trust us to prepare the suite to your satisfaction?'

'I am incognito, Mr Heng. I wish to relax one day or two before we must work. You will grant me this?'

Heng smiled. 'We have completely full booking, Hassan. I grant you anything. Except, Hassan, that you do not put up the fees already agreed. That will give me great problems.'

'We will not quarrel, Mr Heng. Zendik enjoys his stay here. The air suits him—and the company.' Hassan looked over his shoulder and smiled at Miranda. 'You will allow Zendik to be incognito when he arrives?'

'The publicity is entirely in your hands.'

Hassan nodded. 'The divine Maidie is here?'

Heng smiled. 'She is ageless. And she will be pleased to see you, I think.'

Miranda ventured a word. 'She's divine. But Jake's voice is good too.'

Hassan agreed willingly. 'It is the image, Miranda. A singer with red hair and freckles—well, I ask you?'

Miranda understood. Hassan was marketing Zendik, and image was more important than singing skill. It was no use saying that she liked the boy-next-door look. Hassan was into the big time, where image was all. Miranda resolved to herself that she would not judge Zendik on his image, but on his singing. She got down from her stool, and Hassan said, 'Do not leave us so soon.'

'I must change.' She was glad Hassan had arrived. He had distracted her from her problem, the inert Mr Kai lying on the hospital bed, shamming a stroke, she was almost sure. Shamming an illness to focus his family's attention firmly on him to the exclusion of all else.

Hassan was flatteringly attentive. 'See you soon, I hope.' It sounded nice, but she was sure the great Zendik's manager had better things to do than chat to nurses. She was still unconvinced that Zendik was worth a second look. And she had no intention of showing any curiosity whatever.

All the same, she spent a little time with her make-up that evening before she came down. She didn't realise it, but it gave her a glow which her ordinary prettiness didn't have. She chose a dress of black silk, trimmed with gold. It made her feel older, sophisticated more than she really was.

It was good to see Jake already there. He was important to her. Lanky in his jeans, the singer represented a rock, something to cling to when the currents of life became a little rough for her to handle.

He sat next to Miranda, with scarcely a hello. He might have been her brother, and she liked that. He was wearing cowboy boots tonight, complete with silver spurs, but his face was impassive, the grey eyes dull. Miranda forgot her own woes. 'Hello, Cowboy. Meeting someone special?'

'Ah'm joyful, ma'am, joyful.' He emphasised his country accent, looking about as joyful as a leading mourner at a funeral. 'Zendik the great is coming, so we all have to liven up our acts.'

Miranda realised what was happening. 'Ah, I see. Zendik takes the Orchid Room, and we're banished to the Blue Lagoon. Well, no sweat, Jake. The dollars are the same, and you still sing better than he does.'

'I ain't complainin'.'

'Not in words. Jake, there's room for two good singers.'

'Ma'am, I'm a man of the mountains and the prairies. I seen them stags when they meet—both big and strong and good. They have as many miles as you can see to share. But they fight, ma'am, they fight like hell.'

Miranda said quietly, 'But you're a human being.'

'Sure.'

His lugubrious face touched her heart. She leaned over and kissed his rough sandy beard. 'I'm coming to the Blue Lagoon anyway. So is Bill. He won't desert Maidie.'

'Sure,' he said again. And as Suzy came along to serve him, he asked for Bourbon. Miranda hadn't seen him drink whisky before.

Bill and Maidie arrived together, she in a stunning outfit of white buckskin with shimmering fringes, the white stetson bobbing along behind her in time with her pert little steps. It was very effective, Miranda noticed, with a quick glance at all the males in the bar. But it was nice to see that Maidie wasn't impressed when she saw Hassan. He stood up to greet her, but she gave him a perfunctory kiss into the air on each side of his face, and introduced him to Bill. So the great Zendik's magic hadn't touched Maidie either. Miranda just knew he would have no effect on her.

They went through to the Orchid Room for the last time for a season. Miranda noticed that Hassan came through after them, and sat at a table at the opposite side of the room, with three empty chairs. She turned away, and lost interest in the Zendik party. Bill and Maidie were in excellent spirits. It seemed selfish to spoil it by telling them her tale of woe. Mr Kai and his sham stroke could wait.

But it was Bill who brought the subject back to Zendik. He leaned across their table to Jake. 'That must be the Big Man himself, with dark glasses. And there's a white woman with him, wearing a blue kaftan thing. And Hassan, also in a monkey suit.'

Maidie said, when Jake didn't answer, 'The woman is his bodyguard—she's Australian, I think, and a black belt at Kung Fu.'

Miranda just had to steal a little look then at the trio opposite. Zendik was in shadow, so with the dark glasses he could probably hardly see what he was eating. And as she looked, Zendik leaned across and said something to Hassan, who also looked over. Were they talking about Maidie and Jake? She turned away, pretending she had no interest, but the curiosity was mounting as to just why this apparently ordinary man was a super-star around half the world.

Jake stood up. 'Won't be long.' He usually went along to the men's room to tidy up his beard and make sure he was presentable. No dressing rooms or show business fuss for Jake.

Suddenly a tall figure in a dinner suit was standing beside them. Miranda looked up. Zendik was taking off the glasses, and she saw now the deep-set black eyes that drove women wild. They had little effect on her, though she owned that he had a classically sculptured face, a smooth skin and an aristocratic bearing. He gave her a smile that lit up his eyes. 'My name is Zendik,' he said, rather unnecessarily.

Maidie had been deep in conversation with Bill. She looked up at the deep voice, and gave a little squeak of surprise. 'Zen, baby, I thought you wouldn't be here till tomorrow!' She stood up, was kissed lightly on both cheeks, and introduced Miranda and Bill. Bill stood up at once, reverent to a man who had doubled their receipts with the mere mention of his name, and they shook hands.

Zendik said, 'May I sit down?' Jake's chair was free, so Miranda had to nod her permission. He went on, 'I'm happy to meet you, Miranda.'

She did not offer to shake hands. But remembering her manners, she said, 'We've been looking forward to meeting you.'

He leaned forward, the dark eyes intense. 'Am I what you expected?'

She was saved from having to answer by the tall figure of Jake ambling on to the stage in his usual lazy way, picking up the guitar that looked as though it was just lying around where someone left it, and strumming a few minor chords. There was a ripple of applause. Zendik leaned over further, so that he could speak into Miranda's ear. 'Now this man can really sing.'

She turned to him, suddenly alive. 'Yes, I know. I didn't expect—'.

'Me to acknowledge anyone else's superiority? But I must. I was here last year, and Dempsey has a great voice.'

She gave him a smile then. 'Now I know you're a musician! I look forward to hearing you tomorrow.'

Zendik didn't turn away. A smile touched his lips. 'Hassan was right—you are the perfect English rose. I am *very* happy to meet you, Miranda.'

Jake was singing now, starting softly as he always did. She knew he was forcing himself to be cheerful, to sing songs with a lilt to them, that started feet tapping and fingers drumming on tables in time to his rhythm. Zendik too tapped lightly with his fingers, and at the end of the song clapped and cheered with the rest. Miranda stole a sideways look at him. Funny how a megastar looked just as human as everybody else. She admired the generous tribute he had paid to his fellow singer. And she admired those black eyes under the shaggy brows, that seemed to hold hidden depths of fire.

Then the spotlight suddenly shot across the room, and dazzled their table. It was only for Maidie's entrance, but it lingered long enough for people to recognise Zendik, and there was a wild burst of applause for the great man. Maidie was professional enough to let it die down, after Zendik had taken a modest bow, before putting her hat on the white-gold hair and trotting saucily up to join Jake. The applause then was for her alone, and she knew how to make the most of it.

During the duets, Zendik drew his chair closer to Miranda. 'You like it here?'

That was a hard one. She didn't particularly enjoy the work, but one did not burden a perfect stranger with one's problems. 'It's all right,' she said, with a little smile.

'What does that secret smile mean? You're a beautiful creature, Miranda. You remind me of a woodland creature, timid and gentle.'

'Should you speak like that?'

'Why not speak the truth?' He lowered his voice. 'Miranda, I've been married for seven happy years. My wife and children have a beautiful house in Sydney. They know that I travel a lot, meet many people. They know that I talk with other women, dance with them, gamble with them, enjoy my life when I'm away. But there's nothing underhand, I swear to you.'

His sincerity almost blazed from those dark eyes. Miranda began to feel safer, comfortable with him. Star he might be, but apparently one with principles too. She relaxed, and began to ask him more about himself. They chatted so intimately that they did not notice that Maidie and Jake had finished, until they arrived back at the table.

'Getting on well?' Jake didn't sound delighted, but then he never did. 'There's a guy at your table, Zen. I think he wants to talk to you.' Miranda looked over. It was Nigel Croft. How on earth had he managed to get here? He was supposed to be convalescing from appendicitis.

'I'd better come too.' She stood up, and went back to Zendik's table with him, her face stern. 'Nigel, what are you doing out of hospital?' she demanded.

His face fell. 'Sister! I didn't expect to be recognised. I promise I'll get back at once, but I had to meet this great man before anyone else got to him.'

Zendik said gently, 'Miranda, do not worry. Hassan will see him back to the hospital when we have spoken.' He was so very gentle and polite. She thanked him, and went back to Jake and the others.

'He's okay, Jake,' she reported.

'He's not got two heads,' agreed Jake.

Miranda lingered another few minutes. But there appeared to be no chance of getting their opinions about her trouble with Dr Moon. It would do tomorrow. She excused herself, and walked slowly out of the Orchid Room and along the corridor. She heard piano music in the distance, the player who took over when the singers had a rest—the player who had played when she first lunched with Jonathan Smith in Sam's little basement.

'Miranda?' Zendik was at her elbow. 'Have a night-cap with me?'

She widened her eyes. This wasn't a proposition? But no, he was only inviting her to a small table in Suzy's, where they could see what was going on. 'All right, just for a minute.' He smiled, and steered her with a light touch on her arm. She thought how very practised he was, how many women he had charmed like this. But she had no intention of being charmed. She would have a drink with him, because he was a gentleman, and married. But only a little one.

There was bottle of champagne on the table, and two glasses already poured. She might have known! Smiling, she sat down. 'Zendik, you are predictable after all,' she laughed.

'I merely like champagne. And you look the sort of woman who would appreciate a good vintage too.' She had forgotten the black dress, the attempt to make herself look more sophisticated. It had worked.

It was just as she sat down that she saw Jonathan. Zendik was standing, handing her one of the sparkling glasses. The bubbles jumped up from the surface, tickled her nose, and she looked up to laugh at Zendik, protest at the impertinence of his champagne. And Jonathan walked past. He was wearing a dinner suit and black tie. His head was bent, as though in thought. And he was alone.

Miranda half stood. Confused, she only knew she saw a man she wanted to speak to. But he, recognising a situation where two is company, gave a brief nod and hurried past. Miranda was dashed. Of all the people in Genting, she had just seen the only one she would have liked to spend the evening with, and he had just nodded and walked on. That was her answer.

She tried not to watch as Jonathan went down the corridor. She pretended she didn't mind where he went. But the tall figure was blotted out by a group of women on the way to the gambling tables. She heard the excited chatter, in Cantoneon and in English. The Casino closed for one hour, apparently, for cleaning, between three and four, and they were in a hurry to try their luck. Miranda bent her head. Life was enough of a lottery for her, and she had been dealt a few wild cards in the last few days. She smiled up at Zendik as he sat beside her. 'What shall we drink to, Miranda?'

She shook her head. 'In Genting, what shall we drink to but good luck?'

He seemed affected by her cynicism. He reached out a dark, elegant hand, and touched her cheek with his slim, gentle fingers. 'Oh, my dear, yes—to good luck and to happiness.'

'Now that's a butterfly who's very relucatant to be caught.'

Zendik put his glass down. 'How can such a lovely girl be such a cynic?'

'That's common sense, Zendik. It doesn't take very much wit to look around and decide how many of these people are really happy. They're all chasing a dream. Can't you see the look in their faces? Tonight, tomorrow, their dreams will come true. Today there's nothing but searching.'

'Miranda, you are describing life, not Genting.'

'Am I? I wouldn't know. Only here in Genting I've seen things more clearly.'

'You bewitch me, child,' Zendik told her. 'Come riding with me tomorrow. Make some magic among the trees and by the lake for me. They keep two thoroughbreds for me here, you know.'

Miranda shook her head. 'Employees don't go riding. We're on duty.'

'Oh, try. Get Isabel to stand in for you.'

'Isabel?' she queried.

'Da Costa—she's a friend of mine. She was Sister here last year. Tell her that I've at last found a companion who doesn't make eyes at me, who talks sense. That I would like to spend some time with you, Miranda, because you flash into my life like fresh mountain air.'

Miranda was finding that the champagne made her more talkative. She had forgotten she was tired. Zendik was proving a challenging and entertaining friend. 'Most girls make eyes at you, then?'

'You have no idea! I am mobbed, Miranda, so many times. I know it is my living to look—well, sexy—but it costs a lot in shirts. They tear them from my back. There is only one place in Singapore where I buy my silk shirts. Each tour costs me at least two dozen.'

Just then Hassan and the lady bodyguard came along. Suzy immediately was at their sides, before they found a free table. Hassan ordered, then came over to Zendik. 'The orchestra are all here. I've planned rehearsal at eleven tomorrow, if that is okay.'

Zendik nodded. 'She won't come riding, so I might as well rehearse.'

Hassan left them. Miranda asked, 'Do you ride at home?'

'With my daughters, yes. But my favourite sport is motor racing. I have my own grand prix course, where I can break my neck if I like. It is a superb way to get rid of inhibitions, Miranda. Do you drive?'

'Yes, but it isn't much fun in central London.'

Zendik smiled. He had the knack of making his companion feel she was special. Miranda was conscious all the time of a studied line of talk, of questions that had the air of being used before. It should have alerted her, but he did it so well, looked into her eyes with such open sincerity. He leaned towards her. 'If you ever come to Sydney, I insist on showing you the pleasures of motoring,' he told her.

Miranda agreed. 'And now, Zendik, you've spent enough time with a nobody.' She knew Jake would disapprove of that statement, but she had to make Zendik realise that he was wasting his time with her. She just wasn't the jet-set type that he was used to. 'I'm tired, and I have a day's work to do. It isn't a load of laughs, but I intend to do it properly, so I need my sleep.'

'Can I see you up?'

'Thanks, but I have to see the assistant manager about tomorrow.'

Zendik stood up politely. There was no sign at all that he was either bored or annoyed. 'The evening has been a delight.'

She stood for a moment. 'You've been awfully nice,' she told him.

'Against expectations, you mean?' His smile was infectious, and she laughed with him as she turned and went sleepily towards her room.

But she didn't go up the stairs. Still bubbly with the champagne, Miranda went to the front door, and a few

steps outside, breathing in the sweet fresh air. If she went
to bed, she would not sleep, so she walked for a while
along the hotel front. There were people about, coming
and going. Night time didn't mean sleep time in Genting.

She arrived at the hospital and stopped outside. She
knew which window was Mr Kai's. The events of the day
came back to her, the memories of Mary Ann Moon's
harsh face, her hard words and the way she had gathered
the doctors and nurses at the hospital to believe what she
had said—that Miranda Mason was negligent. She
hadn't shared her problem with anyone that day; it was
a burden still on her shoulders alone.

'Miranda?'

She knew the voice. Inwardly she exulted, that fortune had smiled on her. Jonathan Smith was the only
person in the world she really wanted to talk to. She
turned to face him. 'Alone, Jonathan? Where's the beautiful Mary Ann?' She knew the champagne was making
her bolder than normal.

'I don't know.' His voice was low. 'She told me about
the stroke patient. I was watching you. I didn't like to
see you with that man. I thought you might want to talk
about it.'

'Jon—' She felt the poignancy of it all—how she had
wanted to talk to him all day, but dared not. And now
he was here—and if her ears were not playing tricks, he
was on her side. 'Oh, Jon!'

He bent and brushed her lips with his. In a moment
she was in his arms and the kiss was serious and very
wonderful. Somewhere in the background a nightingale
sang. As Jon released her slowly, still holding her close,
a few ragged clouds drifted across the moon. 'You don't
know how glad I am to find you out here. Tell me all
about it, Miranda. We've got all night, and I want to
help.'

He drew her towards a wooden bench under a cherry
blossom tree, and she smiled up at him. 'Well, I did drink

to good luck,' she said, and he pulled her close to him in the warm starlit night.

CHAPTER FIVE

AND SO, though she could hardly believe it, Miranda was finally talking to the one man who could really understand her problem. She had no idea of the time. But Jonathan was at her side, his arm loosely about her shoulders, and she was free to pour out the topic that she had kept bottled up for most of the day. 'I suppose you've been told that I saw Mr Kai and sent him away with antacids when he really had bowel ischaemia?'

'That's about it. How old is he?'

'Early thirties.'

'I've never known ischaemia at that age. But go on.'

Miranda said earnestly, 'Don't try to be nice to me—I want you to be completely impartial.'

'To you? Not easy, Miranda. But I'll try.'

'I'm almost certain that Kai has hysterical paralysis,' she told him. 'He's that type. It was obvious from the way the family clung together. And the way he lay down to be examined—I'm positive that being ill is a way of life for him. But I can't prove it—and also a malingerer might also get something genuine. But I can't prove that either.' She sighed. 'I don't really mind if I've made a genuine mistake—I'm sure most people do—but they were so very unpleasant, talking of suing me, that sort of thing.'

'You told me the night I sat up with you that you were friendly with Cherry Tan,' said Jon. 'Can't you ask her to keep an eye on Kai? If he's shamming, he can't keep it up for ever.'

'She's on Mary Ann's side—I suppose she has to be. No, there's nothing I can do. It's her word against mine.'

'Miranda, I don't think it will come to court. Even if it is a real stroke, you couldn't have prevented it.' He hugged her, and the closeness of him made her so relieved and calm in her mind. She looked up at him, and he bent his head so that her cheek was close to his warm one in the starlight.

At that moment a figure crossed the road. It took their attention at once, because the walk was so crazy. At first he looked drunk, but then it became clear that he was limping badly, and clutching at his stomach. He was coming closer, as if intending to enter the hospital. Miranda suddenly recognised him. 'It's Nigel Croft. The stupid man, getting out of bed so early! It's the appendicectomy Mr Ghosh did the other evening, Jon, the one I stayed with last night.'

She was getting up to give the patient a hand when Jon pulled her back and whispered in her ear, 'This might be your trump card, Miranda. Ask him to watch Kai for you.' He let her go then, and she ran to Nigel, her heart filled with sudden hope.

'Oh, it's you, Florence Nightingale.' Nigel tried to be jolly, but his face creased with pain. 'Don't shout at me. I did what I came to do—I got his signature!'

'Don't talk, Nigel. Hold on to me.' She gave him her shoulder to lean on, and helped him up the step and into the hospital hall. There was no one at the desk. 'I think you're in luck, you truant.' They inched along the corridor to his room, and Miranda smiled when she saw the old trick, a bolster under the bedclothes. 'Get in.'

'Angel of mercy,' he croaked, as she helped him off with his sweater and slacks, and crawled in wearing only underpants.

'Would you spy on the chap in the next room for me? Let me know if he uses his left hand when no one's watching?' Miranda was tense now, feeling sure the night nurse would come along at any moment. But she saw Nigel nod and hold up a thumb in assent, before she crept back like

a thief in the night, clinging to the wall until she reached
the safety of the exit doors.

Jonathan was waiting. 'I've never been involved in such
cloak and dagger tricks before.' He seemed amused—and
pleased when she reported success. 'My dear, I apologise
for Mary Ann. I feel sure she's merely jealous of your
beauty, or she would have consented to an examination in
your presence. It would have been obvious that his plan-
tar reflexes were equal—that would be proof of
shamming.'

Miranda blushed as he mentioned beauty, and was glad
of the darkness. 'I'm terribly grateful for your help,' she
said. 'If I hadn't spoken to you, I would have missed Nigel.
Everything's going to be all right now.'

'I hope so. But Mary Ann still isn't going to like you a
lot, especially if you're proved right. She isn't very keen
on her own sex.' He patted her shoulder. 'I have to get back
tomorrow—I've had a phone call from my colleague. It
seems as though we've got a problem with Staphyllococ-
cus again. These large wounds—even if the nurses are
scrupulously clean, the little bugs seem to get in.'

'Will you—come up again?'

'Probably. I try to come when we have a quiet time.' He
paused, and she heard the nightingale again, answered by
its mate. 'Don't forget what I said—come and see me when
you visit KL.'

'You're going early?'

'Late—I want to catch Zendik's first night. I'll drive
down after that. If I don't see you, little Miranda, I'll be
wishing you good luck.'

'Watch out for the trolls and goblins on the way down!'
she warned.

He laughed. 'Watch out for Zendik!' He cupped her face
suddenly, and kissed her lightly but long. Then just when
she thought he would leave her, he drew her closer, as
though the kiss was addictive, and kissed her again. Powerless to leave him, she stood, close to the warmth of his

body, not daring to put her arms around him, as though it would presumptuous. Suddenly he turned away. 'Hurry, it's getting cold.'

Miranda obeyed, hearing in the background the nightingales trilling. She dared not look round, but she imagined him standing, elegant in his tuxedo, under the ragged moon, with only the nightingales for company. Would he turn and go into the hospital, straight to the doctors' quarters, to his Mary Ann? It was better not to think of that. She must be grateful for his help. She felt secure now in the knowledge that she had someone inside the hospital who would help her. Jonathan had been a tower of strength when she needed one. As she reached the shelter of the Empress, the rain began to fall lightly, whispering droplets in the darkening night.

Next morning she felt calm. She had done what she could. But the job in the medical room beckoned—as boring as bread pudding. Miranda took up her place at the desk, glad of anyone who brought their tiny problems to liven up her day. She amused herself with designing the machine that could take her place—the set questions the patients had to answer with pushes on buttons, and the various slots where plasters, antibiotics or anti-indigestion tablets would shoot out on request.

In the Orchid Room great changes were taking place. The small dais where Jake and Maidie had worked was replaced with chairs for a small orchestra, some of whom turned up early to rehearse the evening's numbers. And the large Steinway grand piano was moved to the front, surrounded by potted palms and clusters of orchids.

Jake found Miranda unashamedly watching. 'Exciting, ain't it?'

'A bit. Have you come to watch too?'

'Sure. I think I'll eat here tonight, move to the Blue Lagoon just for my show. I'd like to see the maestro in action.'

'I guess you're not the only one.' Extra tables and chairs were being humped in by armies of porters. 'I'll eat with you, Jake. I'll come and listen to you too.'

For the first time he grinned. 'Hey, don't be crazy! You have one of the best seats in the house. Keep it. That's an order.'

Silver and blue streamers were being looped up around the chandeliers. Mr Heng was certainly making the most of his international star! Miranda smiled at the thought of being asked to have a drink with Zendik last night. It was really quite flattering. He had seemed so very nice and unspoiled—genuinely Mr Clean. She looked around, secretly hoping that he might notice her when he came down to rehearse, but then the doors were being closed, and the public asked to leave the room. The star wanted his privacy. Jake and Miranda shrugged, and left with everyone else.

Evening dress was everywhere that night—spangled tuxedos, white ones, black ones, scarlet ones and lurex ones. And the women were outdoing each other with the sparkle of diamonds and emeralds, rubies and sapphires. Miranda looked in her box for anything that might look festive enough. She had no diamonds, but she had her gold earrings her father had given her for her twenty-first. They shone in the myriad lights of the chandeliers. She put her hair up over her ears, letting it hang loose behind, then she gazed at her reflection critically. It wasn't often she took the trouble to check her back view, but the hair waved down, and shone with dark brown health, and her dress, low-backed, showed off her creamy skin. It was pink chiffon, she hoped just right for an English rose.

The orchestra was playing smoochy music when the foursome of friends made their way to their usual table. Jake seemed to have got over his moodiness, and accepted the fact the Zendik was king. 'We get a bonus for being chucked out,' he joked.

Maidie said, 'Honey, in show business, you never let nothing bug you. If you did, you wouldn't get far. No, you go along with the Big Ones—and hope and believe that one day you'll be a Big One too.'

'Schmulch but true,' agreed Jake amiably.

A few couples were dancing after the meal, the lights dim, the music muted. But the rustle of excitement started as a spotlight appeared. The dancers went to their seats, and a low drum roll began, then the great man strolled out to a thunder of cheers that set the streamers waving above them. Miranda held her breath. He certainly looked the part. His dark suit fitted like a dream. She noticed the silk tucked shirt—that he had bought in Singapore, and had torn off his back at less respectable venues than the Empress. She noticed the impeccably tied black tie, the shoes reflecting all the glitter around the room in their toe-caps. He was a star, all right, and relaxed and happy about it too. His eyes were as deep and brilliant as the night sky. He looked around the room as someone handed him a microphone, almost making love with his eyes as he smiled slowly at the applause, with slightly lowered lids, holding out his hands to thank them for the welcome. They were already at his feet. The orchestra began to play, and the noise hushed at once. Miranda gazed like a rabbit hypnotised by a cobra, unable to look away.

When she analysed it afterwards, the song was nothing special. It was bland and ordinary. The music was ordinary. It was all about loving and losing, hackneyed, done to death. Yet there was no denying that the emotion was genuine, that Zendik sang with his body and his eyes as well as his voice. Those eyes looked at each woman in the audience as though he sang straight to her. Doubtless he did. It was a masterly performance. And when he turned, and sang the last line directly to their table, it was as though he gazed into Miranda's eyes and her eyes only. She felt tears forming, but could not look away to hide them.

The clapping was deafening. Jake clapped for a moment, then leaned over and whispering, 'I gotta go. Enjoy yourself, Princess.' And as he left, he produced a handkerchief and mopped up the one tear that had escaped her eyelid and was beginning to roll down her cheek.

When Maidie went too, Bill followed her. Miranda didn't move, hardly noticing she was now alone. Ballad followed ballad. There were no gimmicks, just plain, superb selling of a song. In one pause, she noticed that Hassan was crossing the room towards her. 'Alone, Miranda? You are liking the show?'

'Very much,' she smiled.

'May I sit? I looked for you this afternoon. Zen wanted to go riding.'

'He knows that I work,' Miranda explained. 'I can't go away from the hotel.'

'Will you let us know when you are off duty?'

It was flattering to be picked out like that. On the other hand, Miranda realised that most women were with their menfolk, and therefore unavailable for such invitations. 'Where's your lady bodyguard?' she asked.

'Selina? Playing bass.' And yes, there she was, dressed in demure black, holding the large instrument in one powerful hand, plucking at the strings with gusto, the muscles in her arm rippling with strength. Miranda smiled. It was all such fun, so different, almost dream-like. This handsome star, his retinue, his attention to her. . .

Mr Heng came on in person, in sharkskin tuxedo, to thank Zendik for coming, and announce a short break. The pianist came on. Miranda watched him too. He was a nice man; he looked Malay, or possibly Indonesian. He played well. And then there was a pail containing champagne, and their table in near darkness, and Zendik himself was beside her, sipping champagne and asking if she was enjoying herself. Miranda smiled, and replied that she was enjoying herself very much indeed. She too sipped champagne, and the two men discussed the show and agreed that it was going very well.

'Zen, you old rogue, I miss you very much!' Everybody jumped as a large female in a silver kaftan took the fourth seat at the table without being asked. Her voice was piercingly loud, so it was just as well she sat down. She smiled at Zen, and he reached out and kissed her hand gallantly. 'And Hassan too. What villainous things have you been up to since I see you last?'

Zendik said, 'Isabel, love, I've missed you. Have you met the lady who takes your place in the medical room? This is Sister Mason, Isabel. Miranda, meet Sister da Costa.'

She had rather coarse Indian features, but a warm smile. 'Nice to meet you, Miranda. You like the job? I will come back any time—I got fed up with Genting Hotel. Empress much better.' She beamed over at Zendik. 'And I like to be here when Zen is here. We come from the same village in Sri Lanka, you know. My sister used to take him to school.'

Zendik held up his hands. 'No more stories about me when I was small, Isabel! It embarrasses me in front of beautiful women.' He meant Miranda, and she glowed with pride.

Isabel looked at Miranda. 'So, you think this rascal sing well, huh?'

'I do.'

'He sing rubbish the first half—keep best songs till the end, isn't it, Zen?'

'How well you know me!' The great man was clearly used to being teased by this large lady. He gestured the waiter to bring more champagne, and the four glasses were refilled again. 'Well, I might be leaving you—I have made a promise to a young man from London to do a UK tour.'

'My goodness, what an ego! So the adoration of one hemisphere isn't enough for you, child—you want to conquer the world, is it?'

He laughed, enjoying her frankness. 'South-East Asia is chickenfeed. And my wife, she wants to see Britain too. I accepted for her sake.' Miranda thought again that although he was a star, he was also a family man, and obviously not typical of the immoral show business people in the West. She liked Zendik. She sipped again at the champagne, not realising her glass had twice been topped up. He went on, 'And I shall call on Miranda in London.'

Isabel said in a stage whisper, 'Do not trust this man. He is a rogue.' And Miranda briefly remembered that Jonathan had warned her about him too. But they were surely only joking. Zendik was sweet, and quite without false pride.

'I am no rogue, Miranda. I do not smoke or gamble. I drink only when I am working, to relax me. I loathe the idea of drugs. And I made a promise to my father before I left the village. If I become successful, I will not then forget that I am only human, and my success is God-given, and can easily be taken away from me, leaving me with nothing but my self-respect. I made that promise.'

Heng came along then to ask if they were ready to begin again. Zendik turned to Miranda. 'Drink to the second half.' They raised their glasses to each other, and Miranda heard someone at the next table sighing at the touching tableau. She was envied by all women that night, and she gloried in it, strange new feeling that it was.

He made his way back to the stage. Isabel said, 'See how slim and lithe his body is? He keeps fit and healthy. He is a natural singer. I am glad to see how loved he is.'

Miranda found herself blushing as she studied the singer's body as requested. Once she looked, she had no power to look elsewhere. Zendik smiled across at them before taking the microphone and starting the next song. In this half he walked around the room, stopping and singing a little at each table. It was effective, causing much laughter as well as cheering. The women began to take flowers from the tables and throw them to him as he passed them. He came to Miranda's table. Isabel plucked the orchid from the centre of the table, and put it into Miranda's hand, so she had to hand it to the singer. He put it to his lips, and in return took the red carnation from his lapel and gave it to Miranda. She blushed, laughing as the crowd cheered, and clutched the flower tightly against her breast.

And as Zendik returned to the stage for his last song, the lights dimmed again and he was in the spotlight. Two people got up to leave behind Miranda, and as she turned to see them, Jonathan Smith took a step forward, as if to speak. But Mary Ann pulled him quickly back, and the two of them disappeared into the gloom. Miranda had drunk too much champagne to let it bother her, but for a few moments her thoughts were with Jonathan, as he would be getting into a taxi for the journey back to KL and his battle with the Staphylococci. It seemed very far away.

The last ballad faded lingeringly away, and the clapping and cheering began. Zendik left the stage, but came back to barrages of flowers and cheers. Miranda said in Isabel's ear, 'I'm very tired. Goodnight,' and slipped away unnoticed. She felt as though she were floating along the corridor. Tired she was, but also hugely exhilarated by the attentions of the famous man, and by the champagne she had drunk. It was heady, overwhelming. But somehow the memory of Jonathan, coming to tell her something and then withdrawing without saying anything, kept her feet almost on the ground. She was conscious of his warning at the back of her mind, but she was also conscious that she had come for adventure—and here it was. It would be ungrateful to hide, and pretend that she wasn't interested. For one brief moment she had captured Zendik's attention. By tomorrow he would have found another willing companion. She would savour the happiness his company had given her tonight.

She was ready for bed, dressed in her nightie and cotton housecoat, when Bill knocked on the dividing door. 'Are you asleep?' he called.

Miranda opened the door. He also was ready for bed, but apparently pacing the floor, unable to sleep. 'Hello, Bill. You stayed and watched Maidie, did you?'

'Naturally. Was the big guy as good as he's made out? The first number wasn't all that hot.'

'It got better.' Miranda smiled to herself at the under-statement.

'That sort of hype doesn't grab me.' Bill was superior. 'I say, have you any brandy in your fridge? I've finished mine.'

Miranda opened her fridge. She hadn't touched the drinks there. 'There's brandy, whisky, vodka, gin. . .'

'I'll start with the brandy. Join me?'

'No. But I'll talk with you. Something's bothering you?'

Bill drank the brandy. 'I didn't expect to fall in love,' he said ruefully.

Miranda smiled in a motherly fashion as he sat on the edge of her bed. 'Specially with a singer. We're not even musical,' she commented.

'You too, Miranda? You mean—'

'No, look at it this way, Bill. You came for the money, and found adventure. I came for adventure, and found—Mary Ann Moon.'

'Right.' Bill looked down and studied his toes. 'If they stopped paying me tomorrow, I'd still stay.'

'That bad, is it?'

'That good.'

'Bill, you do know that this sort of thing doesn't last for ever. . .?'

'Maybe.'

She looked at him in a alarm. Thinking back, Bill was like her—neither of them had known what falling in love was really like. He had fallen—and badly. Was it good or bad? She had thought she would be the one to suffer first, but although she was enjoying Zendik's attention, she was in love with no one. 'Oh well, enjoy it, Bill. And you can take the rest of the brandy.' He went off to his own room. She didn't bother to lock the door. He wouldn't come to her.

Next day it was still raining, but it didn't matter. They were warm and self-sufficient in the Empress, with plenty to do if they wanted to, and the pick of the best restau-

rants to eat in. Miranda shrugged off the boredom of the
job, realising that the evenings were fun, and that in time
she might get used to doing nothing for a living.

An Indian woman brought her son to the medical room.
He was wheezing, sneezing and coughing. 'We save up
many months for this holiday,' the woman explained.
'Raja he sleep with his brothers and sister. I cannot afford
another room, Sister. You have a bed here, where he may
stay? I will stay to look after him, but I dare not risk the
other children that they catch this cold.'

Miranda was understanding. 'You can have the bed,
certainly. But if I have an emergency, I'll have to give him
back to you—okay?'

There was little chance. The mother agreed with pro-
fuse thanks, and Miranda found that it was quite pleasant
to have company. They chatted together and with Raja.
They ordered squeezed oranges for him, and dissolved
junior aspirins, and exchanged stories of life in their
respective countries. Miranda knew that her sudden interest in Indian village life was based on her friendship with
Zendik. Why not? It was interesting, and it helped both
Miranda and Raja's mother understand more about each
other.

The phone rang. Miranda took it without enthusiasm,
then her face lit up as she heard the fruity tones of Nigel
Croft. 'I say, Sister Nightingale, I can't get out—too many
medical bods around. But I thought I'd better let you know
at once. That bloke in the next room—I saw him doing up
the top button of his pyjamas. I looked in through the pee-
phole. But the point is, I called Dr Moon—well, I had no
choice—she was coming along the corridor. I had to own
up. She seemed pretty furious, but she discharged the fellow.'

'She discharged him? He went away?'

'With all his family, yes. After a while when she examined him again.'

'Wow!' exclaimed Miranda.

'I say, Sister, sorry about letting Moon know. But there was nothing else I could do.'

'You were right, Nigel. I'm grateful to you,' she assured him.

'Bit of a shock, what? Take up thy bed and walk—the poor chap must have got a surprise, thinking he was on to a cushy number. To be kicked out like that—' The voice faded, and then came back. 'Got to rush. Toodle-oo!'

Miranda sat for a moment, Raja and his mother forgotten. She had been right: Mary Ann would hate her even more. But at least she could steer clear of her. But from now on she was pretty sure she would get no more requests to help out in the hospital. Moon wouldn't want her there. Oh well, if Cherry became friends again, that wouldn't matter. But it would make life here even more boring, with not even a hospital night duty to look forward to.

The child's father came down, wanting to know if his wife was coming to dinner in the restaurant. It was getting late then. Miranda didn't mind staying with Raja while his mother went to eat. She wasn't hungry herself anyway, and she didn't want to repeat that excitement of going to the Orchid Room again. She would eat in the Blue Lagoon later, when Raja's mother came back to sit with him. She moved across to the bed. 'Now, Raja, show me all the books you have brought with you.'

'Here they are.' He was a bright little boy, with huge black eyes. Miranda provided a large box of tissues against the sneezes and snuffles, and settled down to an hour of what she enjoyed—cheering up a sick child.

Cherry Tan put her head round the door. 'Miranda, am I allowed in?' She was not in uniform. 'I'm on the way home for a few days off, but I wanted to apologise. I'm ashamed of myself for believing Dr Moon. I feel bad about it.'

Miranda stood up, patting the child's head as he lay sleepily on the pillow. 'Don't feel bad. She is your boss, after all.'

'Yes—some boss! She was in a furious mood because her lover-boy has gone—apparently left her on not very good terms too. And then she had to discharge this Kai, because there nothing wrong with him. You really made her lose face. She will not forgive you for that.'

'I'm not going to lose sleep over her.' Miranda was just glad the affair was over. She smiled at Cherry. 'Have a nice break.'

'I will, thanks. Next time I go down, would you like to come too? I live with my parents and small brother. They would welcome you. I could show you Kuala Lumpur.'

'I'd love that.'

Miranda was left alone with the now sleeping boy. She didn't want to put the light on in case it woke him, so she sat in the lingering dusk, looking out of the window into the shadowy garden. Bill and the others would be getting ready to meet at Suzy's, but she wasn't hungry yet. She would phone for something later, when Raja's mother came back.

There was a rather brisk rap on the door, and she jumped, wondering if perhaps Mary Ann was coming to vent her wrath. She went to the door and opened it, not wanting loud words to distress the boy, but it was Zendik, in dark glasses and casual slacks and shirt. 'Miranda? Why are you here alone in the dark?'

'Just working.'

'Not trying to avoid me?'

'Of course not. Why should I?'

'Why should you indeed?' He pushed at the door. 'Can I come in?'

'Better not—I have a sick child here and the last thing you want is a sore throat.'

'Will I see you in the Orchid Room later?'

CHAPTER SIX

MIRANDA had promised to go to the Orchid Room, but it was only to get Zendik out of the room. She really was tired. It was partly reaction at the glamour of last night, and the drama of Mr Kai ending without any stain on her character. The relief flooded her suddenly with a wave of weariness. All she wanted was a tray of Chinese tea in her room. And as soon as the Indian woman came back to care for her son, Miranda went straight to her room, showered, and lay on the bed drinking tea. It was heaven.

She woke with a start. It was dark, but she had left the bedside lamp on. Her watch said ten-thirty. Yes, the night was still young. She could hear the sounds of voices, distant music, noises that showed that the night life downstairs was in full swing. Wide awake now, Miranda was restless. She decided to go down and see if her friends were still in the Blue Lagoon restaurant.

She took a simple turquoise crêpe shift from the wardrobe. There was no question of jewellery tonight; she was only going down for a chat. She brushed her hair hard, then went down just as she was, with no make-up and casual scandals. She paused at Suzy's, but there was no one there she knew. She went along the corridor towards the Orchid Room, which she had to pass to get to the Blue Lagoon.

The Orchid Room was packed again, with a crowd standing at the doors. Miranda stopped, hearing Zendik's velvet voice from a distance. It made her heart flutter a little to think that yesterday, out of all the glittering array of beauty around her, he had singled her out for special attention. It was something to remember, something to treasure in her secret heart when she was back, tramping the wards in London, or wherever she decided to take her next job. She would buy some of his tapes, and play them, and remember. And yet when she was back in London, it would not be the superficial charm of Zendik that would linger with her, but the blue eyes and magnetic personality of Jonathan Devereux-Smith. He had gone away, yet he had invited her to look him up when she was in KL. And Cherry was going to take her to KL very soon. Now that was something to make the spine tingle a little in anticipation. . .

She was standing at the back of the group at the door. She was hearing Zendik's voice, but thinking of Jonathan. She completely forgot that she had meant to go along to watch Jake and Maidie. Her mind was far away, wondering what sort of clinic he had, whether it was elegant and chic, in a well-off district, or modest outside, excellent inside, like the man himself.

She found her arm suddenly gently taken from behind, and she was turned round to face the dashing figure of Hassan. 'Miranda, where have you been? I look everywhere for you. I go twice to fetch you from your room. Zendik is very mad that you do not come to hear him when you promise him personally.'

Miranda frowned. 'I don't belong to him, Hassan. I have a job to do. I'm sorry if I couldn't make it, but he's hardly without his admirers, is he? You must admit this is a big room. I'm sure one small nurse won't be missed.'

Hassan didn't look affable. 'Zendik doesn't like to be disappointed.'

Miranda laughed. 'Sorry, Hassan, but you make him sound like some big Mafia boss, not a nice, decent young married man. Don't tell me he'll be angry with you if I don't come to listen to him. I'll come tomorrow.' And she turned to walk away, slightly unsettled by the attitude of the young Indian.

'Hi, Princess,' a voice greeted her.

'Oh, Jake—nice to see you. Act over?'

'Yep.'

'Where are the others?' asked Miranda.

'No idea.'

'Come and talk.' They were in the entrance hall now, and she pointed to Suzy's. Hassan had gone ahead of them and was leaning on the bar, chatting to Suzy. Jake agreed. The two of them sat down, and Miranda tried to think of something to say that would take Jake's mind off Maidie's affair with Bill. The elegant Selina came into the bar, and Miranda asked him, 'Do you know Zendik's bodyguard? I'd love to meet her.'

'Over here, sweetheart.' Jake was casual, but he had the manners to get up as Selina approached, Amazonian in her black drapery. 'Like you to meet Miranda, from London.'

'Hi.' Selina was almost a foot taller than Miranda. 'London, eh? What brings you here?'

'A year off. How about you?'

'Actress—not enough parts for tough actresses.'

Miranda smiled. 'You like this job?'

'It was okay when he fancied me.' Selina sat down and drew a lethal-looking cheroot from the folds of her garments, lit it with a flashing gold lighter. 'He don't last long, baby.'

'What?' queried Miranda.

'He's a momma's boy.'

'Oh.' Miranda had no idea what that meant. Selina blew a cloud of fragrant smoke in her direction, and Miranda tried not to cough. So Selina had had an affair with Zendik, in spite of his protestations of angelic innocence. Still, she had probably made the first move. Miranda felt immature about love. Her affair with the houseman at St Thomas's could hardly have been called a grand passion. It had been slightly embarassing for both of them. It had made Miranda decide not to embark on sex without a more definite wish for it. She wondered why being a momma's boy was bad—and decided it didn't matter. 'Oughtn't you to be guarding Zendik?' she asked.

'He's in with Heng, talking business. Heng's man takes care of him there.'

'Heng has a bodyguard too?'

'Sure.' Selina leaned forward, and Miranda tried not to breathe the cheroot smoke. 'See that little guy in the bush jacket? That lump in his pocket's a gun.'

'A gun?'

Selina looked pityingly at Miranda, and suddenly produced a vicious-looking handgun from the folds of her dress. 'Gun—as in Luger.'

'I think I'd rather not know,' said Miranda hastily. 'It seems to make life awfully dangerous.'

'It's no sweat down here. It's in the Casino that things can get hot.' Selina drew heavily on the cheroot. 'They make you laugh, those dudes—make a fuss if a feller isn't wearing a tie, and don't notice the colt under his armpit.' Selina decided it was time to leave. 'He's here,' she said. 'I'd better see him up.'

Zendik came up to them. Was he really mad at her for not going to the Orchid Room? He was wearing his dark glasses, and she couldn't tell. 'You fellows want some caviare? I'm starving! Come on up to my place.'

Miranda looked at Jake, and Selina automatically got ready to follow him. Hassan whispered something to Suzy and joined them, and Jake looked at Miranda. 'Hungry, Princess?'

'I am a bit.' She had missed dinner, being so tired early on.

'Let's go, then.' He unwound his legs, and the two of them followed the trio along to the elevator and up to the best suite of rooms. It was like going into a palace. Zendik walked in casually, accepting the luxury as normal. There was champagne and caviare, cold meats and prawns, rice and salads on a gilt table. Zendik flicked a hand, while Hassan called a servant to begin to hand out the drinks.

Miranda leaned back on a soft velvet cushion, and tried not to be impressed. The chatter was all about audiences, and Jake knew many of the big concerts Zendik had given. 'Lucky we come from different worlds, friend. You can colonise the East, and leave America for me.'

'I'm doing UK next year. Ever done it?'

'Never. Too cold, man. It rains all the time.'

'Prestige-wise it's okay.'

'Sure, if you don't get chilblains.'

Zendik took off his jacket. His silk shirt shimmered in the dim lights, and his slim body was shown off by a wide red cummerbund. He was standing at the table, drinking rather more than he was eating. Miranda was hungry now, but too polite—or bashful—to take too much, so she sipped the wine, and listened, fascinated, to the talk.

The the servant came up, offering her a plate of caviare on tiny biscuits. She tried it curiously, and then accepted more. 'I thought I wouldn't like it, but it's delicious,' she smiled.

Jake was tired. 'Guess I'll hit the sack.' He looked over at Miranda, but she was still eating. 'Don't stay up late, Princess.' And as he went, so did Hassan, Selina and the servant. As if by magic, Miranda was alone with Zendik, and suddenly she felt apprehensive.

He sat beside her on the brocaded sofa, leaning back artlessly. 'Oh, it is so refreshing to relax with someone so sweet and nice. This travelling life means one meets so many artificial people.'

'I can see that,' sad Miranda.

He refilled her glass and took her plate away, nibbling himself at some almonds, and handing them to her. He was, after all, a family man; there was no fear of anything happening. 'You met Jonathan Devereux-Smith, I believe?'

'How did you know?'

'Mr Heng told me. He's a great man, Jonathan. I was sorry he couldn't stay longer this time.'

'He is very—distinguished.' The sofa seemed very yielding. Zendik was very close to her on the soft cushions.

'You meet many distinguished men in London?' he asked Miranda.

'I suppose I do. I work for them anyway.'

'You are very exact, my sweet—so different from most women I meet.' He moved yet closer. 'You think I will enjoy a British trip? You must tell me what to expect in England.' His accent was soft and lilting, his presence disturbing by its closeness. He took the glass from her grasp and took her gently into an embrace that was overpowering by its tenderness. There was no coercion. Miranda made no protest, almost anaesthetised by his words, as he murmured again how very sweet she was. She was suddenly conscious of his masculinity, and realised that was because they were lying together along the length of the sofa. He kissed her then, and murmured her name so that it sounded like the name of a goddess. She tried to think, to make some independent move, but could make no resistance to his strength, and to the increasingly rapid kisses to her face, mouth and neck.

It was when he tried to deprive her of her turquoise dress that she knew what was going on. So far she had pretended that he was different from other men. But it was clear enough what he wanted now, and his dark eyes were even darker with desire, as he succeeded in pulling the simple shift over her head. She wore a cotton bra and white briefs with a touch of lace—she had not developed enough sophistication to choose her undergarments to be viewed by anyone else; only she and her launderette saw her underwear. Until the houseman at St Thomas's. . . And the singer had removed both of these deftly before she had time to wonder what was to happen next. She tried to catch her breath, but it seemed to be out of her control. Zendik's own clothes lay in a heap on the floor, and Miranda found herself wondering how he could treat them that way, considering what they must have cost.

He lay very close alongside her. The perfection of his body was only increased by what she saw and felt—such perfect muscles, taut and firm, and the golden skin, the colour of a Greek bronze. Shame had passed away, and Miranda lay, without struggling against what was happening, but wondering how she could stop it. It somehow seemed not too awful to lie and be embraced by this exotic and magnificent man. He did have a way of making her feel special, even though she thought now that it didn't matter who she was. He was used to having his own way. She ought to have listened to Hassan—he had foreshadowed this violation. Zendik's warm lips wandered over her shoulders, her breasts and body. 'You please me, Miranda. You please me very much.' Between kisses he murmured, 'Your skin is like mother-of-pearl.' And then, very gently, expertly, he entered into her, effectively stifling protest by covering her mouth and kissing her very passionately, beginning at the same time to move within her.

Her mind was overwhelmed. There was no wish for him, yet she didn't find him unpleasant. And now he was moving with too much intensity for there to be time to think. But she knew she must stop him, and tried to twist away. 'Darling, darling,' he groaned, and fell away from her.

Miranda felt tears on her cheeks. This wasn't what she had wanted. She pulled her leg from his golden body, and he sat up, his eyes misty and content. He pulled a silk robe from the back of the sofa. 'Here, my treasure. You can freshen up in there.'

Wrapping the silk round her, she ran into his white marble bathroom, with its circular bath, jacuzzi with gold taps and figures of naked mermaids round the edge. She shook out her simple clothes that she had grabbed from the floor, and caught a glimpse of her white, unhappy face. And she bent her head in shame and anger. Why had she not shouted, protested, screamed? What sort of woman could allow such violation to take place without a murmur of objection? She sat miserably on the floor, tears running down her cheeks, and thought of Jonathan Smith. If it had been Jonathan, she knew there would have been no regret, no misery. She felt like a butterfly, trapped in a spider's web, deformed and ugly by the sticky strands of the web.

Blinded by her tears, she washed herself with the expensive soap, dressed in the clothes that had been forcibly removed from her body—and yet she had made no protest. She brushed her hair, then stood in the midst of the luxury, her hand on the golden knob, not wanting to go out and face him. Zendik could not know what he had deprived Miranda Mason of that night.

He was helping himself to champagne. He wore a silk robe like the one he had given her—it must be the regulation uniform. Her face flamed as she thought of the number of times he must have done this. 'Drink, darling?' He held out a glass.

Miranda stared at him, unable to think of anything to say. She was shattered, completely distraught, yet he offered her a drink. She swallowed hard, opened her mouth to speak, but nothing came out. She had to get away. She ran to the door and let herself out. Even in her haste, she saw that the black-clothed figure of Selina was sitting stolidly outside the door. She said nothing, but ran past her, down the stairs, and along the corridor to her own room, where she flung herself on the bed in a storm of weeping.

In her hysteria, she thought first of Jonathan. He had helped her when she was in trouble last time, but she knew she could never face him again. He had known that this might happen. She recalled the look of relief on his face when he found her outside the hospital. He had thought she was going to Zen's room that night, then. He had been relieved to see she had not. And now—? He would know she was nothing, not worth anything, to give in so easily, where there was no love, no real affection. It was awful, shameful. It was a million times worse than that night at St Thomas's. She had been given no choice—and yet she had given no permission. Zen had taken what she had not wanted to give. Surely that was rape. Yet who could say so, who had seen her happily drinking his champagne, eating his caviare and almonds?

On her way down next morning, after a sleepless night, she found Bill was walking along to the elevator at the same time. He grinned. 'I didn't wake you when I came back at five this morning, did I?'

'No.' Miranda hadn't even looked at the time when she had come home, and the night had been spent with her head hidden under the clothes. She wouldn't have known if the sky had fallen. She wished it had.

'You went to Zen's suite last night? Congratulations—what an honour! But you're a pretty girl, I have to admit that.'

'Really?' Was that all men wanted? A pretty girl? It was apparently all Zendik wanted. 'Bill, are you in love?' she asked him.

'And how!' A blissful expression came over his face. That was the difference: love. Miranda Mason had given herself to a man she did not love. It was not so much the shame now; it was disappointment that she had not found someone wonderful to learn about sex with. She should have known after Trevor at St Thomas's that sex wasn't to be played with. She stole another look at Bill as the elevator reached the ground floor. There was a smile in his eyes. He was truly happy. She turned to her own room, vowing with a vehemence that only she recognised that there would never be a next time, unless she were passionately, devastatingly in love. Unless the man mattered to her more than anyone in the world.

She had forgotten that young Raja was still in the medical room. In a flash the shamed young woman had turned into the professional nurse. Life was going on as normal, and her own distress must not interfere with that. 'How are you, little friend?' she asked him.

'I am well, thank you.' He certainly looked better. Miranda asked the mother if she were willing for him to rejoin his brothers and sister, and the woman agreed, thanking Miranda for being so kind. Miranda watched them pick up their things and take their leave. The job she had despised had at least one satisfied customer. And very soon afterwards, it was Maidie Schumaker who presented herself in the medical room.

'You said stitches out today, ma'am.' She was in cheerful spirits, but Miranda had to force herself to be cheerful, knowing what a contrast there was between Maidie's happiness and her own shame.

'Come and sit down, Maidie,' she invited.

'You aren't your usual sunny self, kid. What's wrong? I heard last night—'

'Nothing to worry about.' Miranda realised that the story would be common knowledge by noon. 'Now, let's look at that wrist of yours.'

'I did all you told me,' said Maidie. 'But it has been painin'.'

Miranda uncovered the wound, and her heart sank. One end was well healed, and three of the stitches could come out easily, but the other two were infected, the skin around them red and swollen. 'Oh, Maidie, this is going to hurt, I'm afraid,' she said.

Maidie widened her china blue eyes. 'Sure? It didn't hurt much when you put them in.'

'You're going to have to think of a whole hunk of chocolate gateau! There's a patch of infection. Sorry, Maidie, but the scar won't be as neat as I intended. This will leave a mark, I'm afraid.'

Maidie didn't look too pleased, but she made no fuss. 'Snip away,' she shrugged.

Miranda did her best. She snipped each stitch with plenty of sloshed antibiotic liquid. The last two were stubborn, and she saw Maidie's lips go white as she tugged them free as gently as possible. Blood and pus ooozed out, and she cleaned it as effectively as she could. 'Shall I get Jake?' she asked.

'He'd pass out!' Maidie could still joke. Miranda replaced the pad with a clean one.

'You must have a full dressing. I can't let you go on with a tiny plaster over this, it would be dangerous. We must make sure this doesn't spread any further.'

'Okay. I guess I can just fool around—tell the audience that the other feller looks worse.' But Miranda knew how the little American loved looking good, and a bandaged arm didn't go with the image.

The moment Maidie had gone, Miranda found her mind going back to last night, to Zendik, his beautiful body writhing in passion, his murmured words of endearment. Words that he must use for so many women. . . She closed her eyes, horrified at what she had done. How she hated—what? Not him. Only what she herself had done.

A woman came in, timidly, her almond eyes apprehensive, and Miranda was again the professional. 'Hello? What can I do for you?' she smiled.

The woman's voice was very quiet, her English poor. 'Sister, I come to tell you—you right.'

'I'm right?' queried Miranda.

'Yes. My *tai chi*—my brother, Kai—'

'Kai?' Miranda's heart jerked. 'He is well?'

'He is well. His—weakness—it has gone away.'

Miranda felt suddenly terribly sorry for the little pale creature; she seemed lost without a brother to look after. She said briskly, 'I'm so glad. You should encourage him to play games—tennis, badminton, that sort of thing.'

The woman's face brightened. 'I will tell him.'

'You should all try to play with him. I think it will help.'

'I will. Thank you, *terimakasih*. You are number one nurse!'

Miranda smiled in spite of her grief, as the woman went out. 'Dr Moon will hardly think so,' she murmured to herself. She sat at the desk, not bothering to close the door the woman had left wide open. She watched the comings and goings in the hotel corridor, and ached within herself.

If only Jonathan were here! yet she did not want him to know her shame. Thank goodness he was away from here, and did not know how easily she had allowed herself to be used. She knew that Jonathan Smith mattered much more to her than anyone else. He was closer to her innermost being than the man who had possessed her body for a few brief unwelcome seconds.

But then someone passed who could hurt her even more. She had thought herself so deep in depression that nothing could make it worse, but then Mary Ann Moon walked past. She walked slowly towards Mr Heng's room, and she paused at Miranda's open door, looking in boldly, tossing her head to make it quite clear that she too had been told about the woman Zendik had taken to his room last night. Miranda half stood, expecting Mary Ann to speak to her, but the young doctor had no such intention. After her knowing look at Miranda, she walked on quickly. There was no point in trying to deny it. Mary Ann knew. . . and Mary Ann intended to let Jonathan Smith know. There was no way she could keep it a secret. Miranda put her head in her hands. There were no tears, her emotions were past crying, too deep for tears. Something priceless had been taken from her without permission, snatched like some worthless toy. And that was what she felt she was herself—a useless toy.

She had no lunch. Instead she went out for a walk. The wind was brisk, and she thought its vigour might blow away some of her guilt. But even that was doomed to failure. She walked past the hospital, out to more open ground alongside the lake, then stood to one side as she heard the sound of horses' hooves behind her, to allow them to pass unhindered. It was a picture that reminded her of a Chinese print, with a spray of cherry blossom bending in a windy sky, and two elegant bays prancing past brushing aside the hanging branches. There was a beautiful Chinese woman on the first horse, looking like a princess in her smart riding outfit, her long hair flowing behind her as gracefully as the horse's tail, as she turned, laughing to her companion. Miranda could not bear to look, as she recognised Zendik on the second horse, needing only a jewelled turban to look like a young Mogul emperor. . .

He gave no hint of having recognised Miranda. She was in the shadow of the trees, and he might not even have seen her in the exhilaration of the ride. The dashing young singer clearly accepted pretty women as his right, and saw no point in prolonging the acquaintance once he had taken what he wanted. Miranda turned, frustration and anger and self-pity bringing tears to her eyes as she walked back to the hotel.

She waited in the medical room for a couple of hours in the afternoon, but there were no patients. She went up to her room, to lie face upwards, gazing at the blank white ceiling, at the slowly revolving fan, seeing nothing, hypnotised by her own deep shame.

She must have slept, for the next thing she knew was a noise in Bill's room—giggles. Maidie must have come to hurry him up for dinner. There was chatter, and more laughter, and then a knock on the door. 'Miranda? Are you ready? Come on down with us—Jake's waiting.'

'I'll be along. Don't wait.' It was surprising how very natural her voice could sound even though her life was in pieces. She got off the bed, flung off her uniform and pulled on a dress, her peacock blue, without bothering to shower. She looked at her wan face in the mirror, and turned away bleakly. What was the point in looking good, only to attract the wrong sort of people?

She was almost pleased, when she approached Suzy's, to hear the booming voice of Isabel da Costa. She was an overpowering lady. With any luck, she would do all the talking, and there would be no need for Miranda to have to make conversation.

Jake was standing up, waiting for her, as though to speak in private before they joined the others. 'Honey, I'm sorry, real sorry,' he apologised.

'What for?' She knew, of course. She saw concern in his eyes.

'For walking out on you last night. I took you along, I shoulda waited.'

'It doesn't matter, Jake. I ought to be able to look out for myself.'

'Not with jackals like him.' Jake was upset, and Miranda felt she had to show him that it was not his fault. 'Honey, I feel real bad,' he told her.

'Don't, then.' She tried to laugh it off. 'Hey, Jake, what's the matter? You think I wasn't flattered to be invited last night?'

He looked into her eyes, and she tried to look back. He saw the tears beginning to fill, and he saw too that there was no point in going on about it.

'Come on, then, let's drink to us.' He drew her along to where Maidie and Bill were still talking intimately together. 'Move over, friend. Make way for the senior partner.' He winked at Maidie. Miranda was the only other person to know that Maidie was two years older than Jake.

Isabel was talking to Heng. Now that was a twosome not to be interrupted, though the big woman broke off her conversation to smile and wave to Miranda. They were talking money—it was impossible not to overhear. But it was too complicated for Miranda, all about percentages and overheads.

'Blue Lagoon tonight, Miranda?'

'Sure, Jake. There are plenty of Frank Sinatra clones around. There's only one Jake Dempsey.' Miranda knew she had managed to brazen it out. It was past history now, except for her own inner anguish. People would forget, but Miranda never would. And how her heart ached when she imagined the pleasure Mary Ann would have, telling Jonathan Smith what had happened, what she had done in full view of half the hotel staff!

Isabel came over. 'Hi, Miranda. Mr Heng said I must ask you first, but I want to come back to the Empress.'

Miranda opened her mouth, but it was Jake who said quickly, 'You ain't kicking Miranda out?'

'No way, Jake. I thought we'd share the job. Same pay, of course.'

Miranda said quickly, 'That's fine with me.'

Mr Heng had been hovering in the background and he came forward then. 'You have no objection? Isabel's old job? I do not mind if you share it.'

'I don't mind either.' The job could hardly be more boring; if Isabel were around, it might liven things up a little. 'Whatever you say, Mr Heng.'

They went through to the Blue Lagoon where the food was just as good as in the Orchid Room. For a little while the four of them chatted, almost like old times, then Jake went off to get ready for his performance. In the distance, the cheers for Zendik could be heard through the open door.

Jake came on, pausing for a second at the table, and patting Miranda's shoulder. She knew he was feeling her sadness with her, and she smiled in gratitude. Jake went up to the front, where a pianist and a bass player came up to join him. They played a little instrumental music, and then Jake went to the front, and gave one of his routine country songs.

The act was going well. When Maidie went up to join him she got her usual burst of applause, and Miranda only then noticed that Maidie had removed the bandage, and had only a tiny strip of plaster over her wound. She was concerned at once, because the lower end of the cut had been quite badly infected. She had not given antibiotics by mouth, because Maidie had promised to keep the sterile bandage on.

Still, she could talk to Maidie later. Her vanity could cause trouble, but she was certainly a staunch little trouper, and as she sauntered to the front, the spotlight surrounded her, highlighting her shiny blonde curls. She was smiling broadly, her blue eyes showing how she loved performing.

Suddenly she faltered, half turned towards Jake, holding out her arms. Then she fell. The audience rose, with gasps and cries. The music stopped, and Jake picked her up, totally unconscious. Miranda had rushed out at once, and now examined the still form. The redness that had started at one end of the wound now covered the whole forearm. 'Jake, get her to the hospital at once,' she said urgently. 'The infection has a hold. If it gets into her bloodstream, then it could be terribly serious.'

Jake waved away a stretcher. With taut lips, he snapped, 'I'll take her.'

CHAPTER SEVEN

In the Japanese Lounge someone was playing the Steinway. It was afternoon, and Miranda and Bill had been at
the Empress for two months. She had seen two patients in
the morning, then relinquished the medical room to Isabel. She had taken to wandering out in the afternoons,
venturing further afield, both to avoid meeting Zendik or
any of his cronies—and to find privacy to cry a little away
from prying eyes. She knew very well she was suffering
from reactive depression, but she was trying to get over it
without treating herself with anti-depressants.

It was silly. Most girls would have taken a night with
Zendik as a compliment. But for Miranda, she felt that
her feelings for Jonathan were so strong that it was wrong
for her to have allowed anything to happen with anyone
else. In her own way, she had been unfaithful to her own
feelings, her own inclinations.

She came in from the road when she heard the Steinway. It was the same pianist she had heard all through her
days here—first in Sam's basement. He had played for
Zendik too. And when he felt like it, he played in the
lounges. She crept silently into the lounge and sat down.
There was no one else there; he was playing for himself.
And she realised why the music had drawn her indoors—
he was playing a simple Mozart sonata that she had
learned from the village piano teacher in Alston Magna,
all those years ago.

She didn't at first recognise the symptoms of homesickness; she thought the stirrings of sadness within her were
part of her depression. All she knew was that those tinkling notes, so beautifully played by someone who thought

he was alone, brought back strong memories of a sunny afternoon in her father's vicarage. The ancient french windows had been forced stiffly open because of the unexpectedly warm day, Miranda was sitting under the apple tree in the corner of the overgrown lawn, and the church organist had picked up her music and played it on their old yellow-keyed piano. He had brought a beauty from the piece that Miranda's struggling fingers had not been able to discover.

For a moment she forgot where she was, lost in memories so strong that she could smell the fragance of the apples, the warm grass. And then a group of guests came in, laughing and arguing after a game of tennis. The spell was broken. She was in the Empress Hotel, a mile up into the clouds of Genting, alien, friendless. . . At least, she had friends, but she felt uniquely alone at that moment. And she wondered, in her sadness, whether to telephone Jonathan. It was too far to phone Alston Magna—and anyway, they would only just be getting up in England. Jonathan was the only other person in the world she knew she wanted to be close to. And yet one did not phone a surgeon when he might be operating. She sighed, her heart aching within her as the Mozart went on. What would she say to Jonathan if she did reach him?

Someone came into the lounge and sat down also in silence, listening to the music. Miranda didn't expect anyone she knew, so kept her face averted, hiding the tears which she knew were brimming, waiting to fall. But then someone pushed a handkerchief into her hand, and she turned as the tears rolled down her cheeks. 'Maidie! You're out of hospital! Oh, I'm so awfully glad. Are you feeling all right?'

'I feel wonderful.' She looked into Miranda's face. 'Hey, honey, it ain't your fault. Don't look so gloomy.'

'Septicaemia isn't funny, Maidie.'

'And whose fault was it? Mine, for taking the bandage off, messin' around instead of leaving it be, like you told me.'

'I should have checked more often,' Miranda persisted.

'Honey, don't! And don't cry, please. This music means somethin'.'

'You're very pereceptive, Maidie. It reminds me of home—our big old uncomfortable vicarage. . .'

'Honey, troubles turn out to be all for the best. You learn from them, and come through smilin'.'

'I've no troubles, Maidie.' She tried to make her voice natural.

'Honey chile, I ain't blind.' Maidie moved closer and lowered her voice. 'I guess you hurt bad because of the way you was brought up. Life here is—well, freer, I guess. Can you see Zendik and Hassan the hustler in your village? Can you see me and Jake, for that matter?'

Miranda managed to laugh as Maidie wiggled her hips and ran her fingers through her fairy-gold hair.

No, the four she mentioned would not blend into the countryside of Alston Magna. But Jonathan would. . . Mummy would like Jon. 'You've known Zen quite a while?' she asked Maidie.

'Yes. We're pretty mad at that dude. I told Bill he ought to speak to him, but he won't because he's management, and management think Zen is kinda out of sight money-wise.'

'I can't forget it, Maidie,' Miranda sighed.

'Honey, why don't you take a break away from here? I think you need it. Isabel is doin' the work. You started too keen, tried to get into a new way of life too soon. Now I say you gotta relax, before you hurt so bad you can't get over it.'

She spoke so quietly, so matter-of-factly. Yes, Maidie had been around some years, and she couldn't have looked so good if she hadn't learnt how to take the knocks. 'You're very wise, Maidie,' Miranda agreed. 'And I think you're quite right. Cherry Tan has invited me to KL for a few days. I said no, but now I see that if I stay here I'm just going to be miserable.'

'Atta girl! We'll miss you, but I just know you need to go.'

'I'll speak to Cherry when she comes off duty.'

Maidie stood up. 'Great! Catch up with you tonight, honey. Now where's that Dempsey got to?' And she bobbed out of the lounge, almost as chirpily as normal. She had been ill for some weeks, and it was nice to see her going back to Jake first, and not Bill. That was important to see.

The pianist had finished the sonata, and was now playing The Blue Danube with some gusto. Miranda felt confidence rushing back to her limbs, giving her back strength and optimism. Maidie was sweet. The music came to a flourishing conclusion, and Miranda clapped her hands enthusiastically. The pianist turned and grinned at her. 'Thanks. You're the best audience I've had all week.'

'You're very popular. I've seen you,' answered Miranda.'

'Not many people applaud this kind of stuff. It's what I like to play, but I can't very often.' He had a nice smile, curly greying hair, a hint of Australian in his accent.

'Does it make you homesick too?'

He looked surprised. 'I haven't really got a home. But I suppose in a way. . . forgotten dreams, if you like. . . starting out thinking you're the greatest.' He smiled ruefully. 'Funny how a little Austrian guy with a crazy lifestyle gets you right in the guts, isn't it?'

Miranda laughed. 'I've never heard Mozart called that before! You put it very well.'

'Thanks for listening. I mean that.'

'I suppose Mozart has sorted his problems out by now.' She found it was easier to smile now than it had been an hour before.

'I guess that's right. But a pretty kid like you can't have any problems. Oh, I get it—homesick, huh?' He patted her shoulder. 'You're lucky to have a home to miss.'

'Well, if you put it that way—' They smiled as he went away. Miranda watched him go, still not knowing his name. Yet she had admired his playing since her first day here. Funny how you meet people you share some little things with. . .

Miranda waited until she thought Dr Moon would not be about before she went across to the hospital to find Cherry. It was strange and rather pleasing to find that she was no longer nervous about meeting Mary Ann. She felt she had grown up since being in Genting. Each day that passed made her feel more philosophical, and less childishly apprehensive about life.

'Hi, Cherry. You off duty?'

Cherry was just tidying the desk. 'Hi there—nice to see you. You have kept yourself to yourself, haven't you? Okay now?'

Cherry knew too. But Miranda didn't mind. She had the Zendik affair more under control now, knew that it meant very little to anyone else but herself. 'I'm fine, Cherry,' she smiled, 'but I need a holiday.'

'You mean you'll come down with me? That's great. I'll phone Mama right away. You'll enjoy the big city, Miranda, I promise. Shopping is much more fun with two.'

There was another female voice from the dimness at the back of the hall. Mary Ann Moon was just coming down the stairs into the foyer. 'Isn't everything?' She came into the light. 'Oh, it's you, Miranda.' A coolness came into her voice, but she wasn't quite so aloof as she used to be. 'Where are you going shopping?'

Miranda answered, glad to feel confident and untroubled by the other woman, 'Kuala Lumpur. I'm going down with Cherry next weekend.'

Cherry picked up a pile of files. 'Wait here, Miranda. I'll just pop down and put these away.'

Miranda thought Mary Ann would go away then, but she lingered. 'You haven't spent much time in the heat, have you? Better not to go mad on your first day down. You feel okay, but you might get heat exhaustion. Take my advice and go very easy for a day or two.'

'Thanks, I will.' So Mary Ann could be pleasant when she chose.

'And you'll take anti-malarials, won't you? Here, I've got some in this room. Take a couple now, and another two this time next week. Easy dosage, and you'll be completely protected from malaria.' She opened a small drawer in the desk with a key, and gave Miranda a bottle of white tablets. There was a water cooler in the hall, and she encouraged Miranda to take the first two at once. 'Better safe than sorry. People with fair skin do seem vulnerable to mosquitoes.'

'You're very kind. I hadn't thought of that. We were warned in England to get medical advice if we were going to travel away from Genting. Thanks.'

'You're welcome. Have a nice time.' And Mary Ann Moon went off towards the wards, her white coat floating behind her, her dark hair beautiful in the dim light.

Miranda met Isabel in Suzy's that night, and her fellow Sister was quite delighted to take over full-time for a few days. 'You should see something of the country,' she said, 'Malaysia is a place of many surprises. Pity to sit on top of a mountain for a whole year. Find some beaches, buy some silks, have your fortune told by the best astrologer in the world.'

'I'll do just that.' Miranda was feeling better, and grateful to Maidie for coming to talk to her just when she had needed it most.

The four of them had a sling together, and then went along to the Blue Lagoon as they had not done together since Maidie's illness. It was almost like the first happy days—but not quite. Miranda knew why. She had grown up a bit, and she was no longer the wide-eyed kid, eager to see a new country, that the others had treated rather protectively. She was more of an equal now. It was cruel that it had taken a near-rape to make her so. She ignored the sounds of Zendik's cheering audience as they passed the Orchid Room. She could never forgive him for what he had done—yet she knew within herself that her own sheer ignorance had prevented her from stopping him before it was too late.

Jake and Maidie told her of the places in the city they knew. But they had spent most of their time in the big hotels, and Miranda wanted to see the Malay shops and some of the tourist sights.

By the time the two nurses were humping their bags into the taxi that was to take them down to Cherry's home, Miranda had been told so much about the city that she decided she could probably find her way around on her own. But she recalled Mary Ann's advice, and knew she must be careful at first.

The heat was in fact the first thing she noticed. The taxi was air-conditioned, and when they reached the bottom of the winding road, he switched it on. At first Miranda felt too cold. But when Cherry lowered a window, letting the heat in, she understood why he had done it. The changeover of temperature was abrupt and unsettling. But when Cherry insisted on getting out of the taxi to buy mangosteens and rambutans from a thatched wayside stall, Miranda was glad to come and help her choose good ones. The air was like being in a warm bath. Sweat started on her forehead the moment she got out of the taxi.

She was fascinated by the outskirts of the city, the small shanty houses and the narrow tree-lined roads. But the big sprawling metropolis had spread out far, and modern homes and tall concrete blocks were soon in evidence, as well as masses of new buildings in the orange-red earth, showing increasing development and prosperity. Cherry said, 'You are lucky. We go through the centre of town to get out to the suburbs where we live. You will see the main sights on the way.'

And because Jonathan Devereux-Smith was seldom out of her thoughts, Miranda asked, 'Will we see the Devereux Klinik?'

Cherry spoke a few words of Malay to the driver, and he nodded. The middle of the city was a jumble of ancient and modern, but soon the golden domes of the municipal buildings were clear against the bright blue sky. Cherry pointed out the Selangor Club, 'Very exclusive,' and then the *padang* in front, where all important cricket matches are played, and functions also, if they were not too large. The really big ones were in the Merdeka Stadium nearby.

'And there is the Klinik,' she added.

'Where?'

'Behind those big banyan trees.'

It was a modest white building. The brass plate was small—typical of Jonathan, the man who never sought the limelight. Miranda felt suddenly enormously happy. It wasn't home, but it felt like it. Now she knew she was near to him, and it didn't matter too much that he was unaware of her presence. She at least knew where he was. It seemed to fill a great void in her life.

They went on through the city to the leafy suburbs. Cherry's home was simple but elegantly furnished. She had a smaller brother who was still at school; her mother was a housewife now, but her father was a schoolmaster. They made Miranda very welcome, insisting on her eating much more than she intended of the delicious seafood and noodles. The atmosphere was very hot, in spite of the fan and the air-conditioning. When Tai Chi, the brother, came home, he switched on the TV. Miranda felt suddenly terribly tired. Mrs Tan was kindly, and showed her the coolest room under the bank of flowering frangipani. 'Turn the fan up to the highest, then you must sleep. Feel better tomorrow, and see something of the town.'

When Miranda woke, it was already after nine in the morning. Cherry had brought her a cup of tea, and Miranda was ashamed of sleeping so long. 'I suppose it must be the heat,' she said. 'Mary Ann did warn me.' She took the cup, and saw that her hands were shaky. Surely she couldn't have a fever? She had seen no mosquitoes yet, and she had been taking Mary Ann's tablets. When she had drunk the tea, she leaned back on the pillows, feeling utterly exhausted. 'This is ridiculous! I haven't been here five minutes. I can't possibly be suffering from the heat.'

'No, I don't think so. But we'll stay in if you like,' offered Cherry. 'My school friend is coming round, so we can stay home and chat.'

Miranda felt bad. The school friend was coming round to go shopping with them and she would spoil it if she didn't go. Making an enormous effort, she swung her legs off the bed. 'Give me five minutes, and I'll be ready to go.' She showered, hoping that the cool drops would help to waken her, but they only made her feel dizzy, and she had to sit down on the bathroom stool, holding her head between her knees. What an awful thing to happen, spoiling everyone's day! She waited as long as she could, before dressing in the lightest cotton dress she possessed. Cherry had laid out cereal and fruit for breakfast, and Miranda managed to eat a little, though she had no appetite.

She knew very well that there was something wrong. But she was usually healthy, and decided that whatever was the matter with her, it would probably go away once she started to enjoy herself. Cherry's friend lived nearby, and she was at the door within minutes.

'This is Sue,' Cherry introduced her. 'She is a secretary to a millionaire. He owns some of the shops, and we will get discount on everything you want.'

'Where are these shops?' asked Miranda.

Cherry smiled. 'Not far from Mr Smith's place, Miranda, where I took you yesterday. We'll do some shopping, and then Sue wants to take you to our favourite restaurant.'

Perhaps in was the mention of Jonathan that gave her the extra energy to go out into the hot sun with them. He head felt as though it were floating somewhere far above the rest of her body, but she managed to follow the others round the shops, praise the clothes they bought, and show some enthusiasm for the exotic goods in the little bazaars. 'I must come here before I go home, and get souvenirs for all my friends,' she decided. But she was not inclined to buy anything she would have to carry; it was enough work carrying herself in this weak state. As if in a dream, she followed the others, hardly noticing where they had got to.

'Miranda, do you mind if I pop into that office with Sue?' Cherry asked. 'One of our friends works there, and I always like to say hello.'

'Of course not. I'm dying for a sit-down.'

'Then I'll put you under the banyan tree, where you can see Jonathan Smith's clinic, okay?' Cherry was laughing, but she didn't realise how much Miranda felt reassured and contented to sit within sight of Jon's door. 'Back in five minutes, Miranda, and then we'll take you for the best *nasi limak* in town.'

Sitting down, Miranda felt fractionally better. She was in the shade, comfortable, and in no rush to get away, least of all to eat. And from where she sat she could see the sun glinting on the brass plate outside Jonathan's clinic. She leaned her head back and closed her eyes, perfectly content to stay where she was for the next ten months. Then she could meet Bill at the airport and they could fly back to reality. She felt her head grow light, but had no strength to lean over and put it between her knees. She was drifting away, light as a feather, drifting somewhere up into the branches of the huge banyan trees, where all was peaceful and soft as cotton wool. . .

She came back to consciousness as mistily as she had left it. The surroundings were all white, just as she had thought when she decided it was cotton wool. But the smell was different—clean, antiseptic, not the city fumes and the smell of the hot grass and the banyan tree. And she was lying flat on a hardish white sheet, smooth and shiny to the touch. Somewhere in the background she could hear the squeak of a fan, the whirr of its blades. She closed her eyes. It was far too much trouble to think. . .

And then a voice sounded in her ear that would bring her back from the jaws of hell. In her imagination she heard Jonathan Smith, and his voice was infinitely beautiful, gentle and caring. 'My poor sweet darling!' That was a nice thing to dream, and she waited in her sleep for more. There was a cool professional hand touching her brow. That must be Jonathan too. This was the sort of dream she could live with for ever.

Deep, deep in the cotton wool, she waited, content. Then Jon's voice again, muffled, as it would be if they were both inside cotton wool—'Look, you go. I'll do the BP again, and try to get through to her. I'll call you if I get anything.'

Miranda opened her eyes, and yes, his vision was there, just as she had hoped, the blue eyes as blue and as beautiful as ever. But they were serious now, not crinkling at the corners. He bent over her, took her hand that lay limp on some sort of coverlet. 'Miranda darling, can you hear me? It's Jonathan. You've just been brought in as an emergency. I never had such a shock, to see you lying there, so pale, so very ill!'

She knew it was only a dream, and you can never speak in a dream. All the same, he looked so concerned that she had to try. 'Where—where's Cherry? She left me—on a bench—' Her voice was there, very weak and husky.

'That's where we found you, in a coma. You hardly had any blood pressure. Just let me try it again. I've taken some blood for analysis, dear. We can't find out what's wrong with you.' He wrapped the cuff of his sphyg around her arm. Miranda couldn't explain that she was perfectly content, in no pain, as long as Jonathan stayed with her, looked after her.

'I think—' she cleared her throat, 'isn't it just heat exhaustion? I was warned that I might get it.'

He shook his head. 'I don't think so—the coma was too deep. Let's hope so, though. It means that in twenty-four hours you'll be well again.'

Miranda tried to sit up suddenly. 'I *am* in your clinic! I thought I was dreaming it.'

Jon managed a smile at her sudden realisation. 'Yes, Miranda. Please sit still while I check your BP.'

'Sorry.' She lay back again, trying to fathom the wonderful position she was in. 'What's the reading?'

He undid the cuff. 'Very low, very low. And you're developing a fever. I can't figure this out, Miranda, but I've got my physician colleague to come over and advise me.'

'I can't stay here,' she protested. 'I can't afford—'

Jonathan put his fingers over her lips. 'Twenty-four hours, my dear. We must get to the bottom of this.' His hand was cool and lovely, and she wanted him to leave it there. While he was there, there was absolutely nothing wrong with the world, except the simple problem of not having the strength to get out of bed. He appeared to hear her unspoken wish, and smoothed back the hair from her forehead. It was wet with sweat, but the touch of his fingers made it all right. He bent towards her, and whispered, 'I don't know how you got here, Miranda, and I don't know what's wrong with you. But you mustn't worry about anything. I'll care for you. You don't leave here till you're well again. And not another word about money— I forbid it.'

Miranda listened to his words, so honey-sweet, and suddenly she felt tears welling from under her closed lids. If he would only hold her in his arms, then she knew all would be well. But instead he patted her hands, then stuck a thermometer under her tongue. She felt herself drifting back into unconsciousness before he took the thing out— and then she was suddenly seized by a fierce fit of shivering. The thin sheet over her seemed both hot and very cold at the same time, and she heard Jonathan's keen intake of breath, as his arms came round her to try to stop the violent shaking.

The other voices drifted into her consciousness. She heard Cherry and Sue talking to Jon. Suddenly too weary to listen, she heard words that ought to alarm her, like malaria, and mosquitoes, but she was too washed out to be scared. She retreated into restless sleep, lost count of time.

She had no idea how long she was in delirium. The room was dim all the time, the temperature even. Sometimes she was washed down, her hair combed by gentle nurses. Sometimes she heard male voices discussing her blood pressure in hushed tones. And sometimes she knew Jonathan was there, because she felt calmer, at peace, and more alive as she waited for his hand to touch her, his lips to be near to her face as he spoke gentle words to her when no one else was there.

Then one day she opened her eyes and her vision was clear. Cherry was at the foot of the bed, holding a bouquet of orchids. She looked anxious, and Miranda was glad she could speak properly, tell her that she felt okay. 'I haven't told Bill,' said Cherry, 'but he'll wonder why you aren't going back on time.'

'Good. I'm glad you didn't tell him. No point in him worrying when he can do nothing, and I'm in the best hands.'

'Lucky we were near the clinic when you passed out. Mr Smith has been awfully good,' Cherry told her.

'You don't have to tell me!' She would never forget his care, his concern for her. 'Leave Bill to me, I'll telephone him when I've had a word with Jonathan.'

'Okay, Miranda. I have to go back tomorrow, but Mama will come and see you. She sent these flowers for you.' Miranda was touched by the kindness of virtual strangers.

Next morning she woke with no temperature. She ate a little breakfast. This was fine. Perhaps she should have gone back with Cherry. But no, she felt faint the minute she tried to stand. She leaned back on the pillows, puffing. For the first time in her young life she began to wonder if there was something dangerously wrong. What would dying feel like? She closed her eyes, and tried to imagine what it would feel like to know that the next breath would be her last. Truth to tell, she felt too weak to care much. But Mummy and Daddy would. And Bill. And Jonathan, maybe—

'Miranda?'

She opened her eyes and smiled at him. 'That's my name.'

'I know. It says so on the door.'

For a moment they exchanged a smile of remembrance, of the day he had come to the medical room at the Empress and took her to lunch leaving Mary Ann in the sauna. Jonathan came and sat on the bed. 'It's good to see you smile.'

'I feel a lot better,' she told him.

'It's the temperature that's come down. But Dr Subamatu is puzzled. There were no parasites in the blood.'

'Well, I'd been taking anti-malarial tablets, so I could hardly get malaria.'

'Do you know the name of them?' His voice changed.

'No. But Mary Ann gave them to me.'

'Mary Ann?' He went to the door. 'Get me the hospital at Genting at once—Dr Moon.' He went out, saying to Miranda, 'Excuse me for a moment. We might be on to something.'

When he came back, Dr Subamatu was with him. He was holding a piece of green paper, which he showed Miranda. 'You see? The alkaline phosphatase is very high, abnormally raised in all three tests we have done. Dr Subamatu wants to take you down for a liver scan. Do you feel up to it?'

Miranda was checking her full blood count. Yes, the test showed that there was some malfunction of the liver. Hepatitis? Where would she catch such a thing? She gave the paper back. 'Of course. I'm being an awful nuisance.'

'No more of that, my girl. Into the chair, if you can manage. Sonia will take you down for the scan.' And Jonathan helped her into the chair, almost carrying her in his strong arms, as her legs refused to hold her. For a moment she rested her cheek against his chest and felt the throbbing of his heart, and then she was on the way along the corridor in the wheelchair, again feeling lightheaded and not quite orientated. What could be wrong with her liver?

Jonathan was still in her room when she returned from the ultrasound scan. It had been painless, and gave an instant reading. The liver was apparently normal in outline. Jonathan seemed sure then. He sent the nurse away, and sat on the bed. 'Well, Miranda, I think I've solved your problem. Mary Ann told me which form of quinine she gave you. I checked with the central Lab in KL and the stuff you were taking has hepatitis as one of the commonest side-effects. When did you take your last dose?'

'Just before coming down from Genting.'

'In that case, my dear, you should get better and better each day, as the body gets rid of the accumulations.' He reached out and squeezed her hand. 'Let's keep our fingers crossed—you won't need any more treatment. Just rest and get better. But it hasn't been a very pleasant experience for you. What a way to enjoy your first holiday!'

'I don't mind.' Miranda kept her eyes down, hardly able to tell him how much she had enjoyed being cared for by him. 'At least next time you'll be aware of this side-effect. I may have stopped someone else from going through this. And Jonathan, thank you for—' He stopped her mouth with his hand.

'No thanks are needed. I'm glad it was here where I could look after you.'

'How can I show my appreciation if you won't let me thank you?'

He smiled. 'We're madly busy in Surgical. Perhaps you could come and do a bit of night duty for me, next time you feel like a break from Genting?'

'I will. I'd love to.' She lay back, feeling tired after the conversation, but cheered by the news that she would soon be better—and delighted by Jon's invitation to work for him. She would take him up on that the minute she had made arrangements back in Genting. She felt her heart beat faster at the idea, and knew she was getting better now, by the minute. She gave a little bounce of excitement

as Jon left the room. He would be surprised by the speed
with which she got better and returned as his employee!

CHAPTER EIGHT

IN another couple of days Miranda felt strong enough to telephone Bill to send a hotel car for her. 'Are you sure you're all right? he asked anxiously. 'I was so scared when Cherry told me what had happened. You haven't told your folks?' Bill's words tumbled out in his relief.

'I'm quite well. Just a bit weak, but good as new, Bill. How are Jake and Maidie?'

'Fine. Missing you. It seems a long time since we were all four together—first Maidie was ill, and now you. Hurry up and come back to normal.'

'Well, I'm not sure about that.' But she said no more about her plan to go down and work in the Devereux Klinik. All the same, before she left she paid a visit to Surgical, met Sister Leonie who was in charge, and mentioned her idea. Leonie sounded willing, and showed her the wards, and the comfortable nurses' home nearby, with a view of the gold domes of the municipal buildings. Miranda promised to give them a call when she was available. And then it was time to fetch her bag, and go to the waiting hotel limousine at the front door. She went to look for Jonathan to say goodbye, but was told he was operating. Oh well, she would write him a little note of thanks—though nothing could really make up for his wonderful care and devotion.

It seemed a very elegant car for a hotel taxi, but then she remembered that there were different grades of vehicle, depending on the importance of the guest. As a friend of Bill, she was in the management class. She smiled as she stepped into the open door. It was nice of him to give her the best. The chauffeur closed the door, and Miranda settled herself and her bag. Then she gave a little cry of surprise. There was a man sitting in the opposite corner, and as he turned to face her, she saw that it was Zendik.

For a moment she could think of nothing to say. The chauffeur closed the dividing glass, and slid smoothly out from the Klinik entrance into the main stream of traffic. Miranda didn't notice, so shocked was she to see Zendik. He sat there, wearing a black silk shirt, his black eyebrows and aristocratic nose reminding her of a brooding eagle. And she felt ill at the memories he revived within her. She looked again at the limousine as it purred smoothly on its way to the suburbs. Yes, even for the Empress, this was far too magnificent. 'It—this must be your car.' Her voice was halting. She had never wanted to see him again at such close quarters.

'Yes, one of them.'

'But—'

'I know you didn't want me. As soon as I heard of your illness I wanted to do something. And then—' he looked down at his hands, as nervous as a schoolboy—'I have been very wrong, thoughtless—Miranda, it is not in my nature to want to hurt anyone, truly. I had no idea. I want you to forgive me.'

Miranda couldn't speak. He was right—it wasn't in his nature. He was a gentle soul, and would have left her if she had asked. No one would have let the episode mean so much—most women would have given their eye teeth to have been in her place.

He spoke again, very softly. 'I genuinely thought—I mean, most Western women—are not like you—I thought—'

She interrupted him, looking him in the face, knowing that it was part of her growing up to be able to accept his apology and forgive him. 'Zen, let's forget it. Water under the bridge, that sort of thing? I was as much to blame, and I was a bit out of my depth, with all the champagne, the food, all that.'

He said, 'Yes, but I should have seen that.'

Miranda checked to make sure the glass partition was properly closed, then she turned to the singer, and suddenly he looked quite normal, not like a bird of prey at all. 'Who told you? You could have had no idea unless someone told you how miserable I was. And I was miserable with myself, not you. It was Maidie, wasn't it? Or Jake. You know them quite well. It must have been Jake.'

His slim dark fingers were still twisting together in uncharacteristic nervousness. She put out a hand, and put it over his, to stop them. As she took it away, Zendik faced her, saw there was no blame in her eyes, and shrugged with a hint of a smile. 'Jake doesn't get violent very often.'

'Did he tell you off?'

'He did.' They were nearing the Batu caves on the outskirts of the city. The cliff face raised up, blocking out the sun. Zendik said, 'He told me that people in our profession get big-headed, out of touch, and he was right.'

Miranda felt calm enough to smile with him. 'I guess there aren't too many modest violets in your line of work.'

'Thanks for being so nice. I hope we can be friends properly now.'

The thought of returning to the Empress, to the Genting heights, even at peace with herself, did not appeal. She knew she was able to be so calm and detached with Zendik because she was already planning the rest of her year down at the Devereux Klinik. She would be working with Jonathan Smith. She had no intention of hanging around bars, seeing two patients a day, wasting time idly when she could make herself really useful and spend the time with someone she admired a lot.

They were beginning the climb now, up the side of the mountain. At first it was not too steep. There were thousands of bamboo trees at the road's edge, making that characteristic design against the afternoon sky. And then there was a flash as Miranda saw her first Flame of the Forest tree, vivid and beautiful among the shades of green and brown. Zendik said, 'You are very quiet, Miranda. You are properly well again?'

'Yes, thank you.'

'I should thank you for making me a wiser man. I will see women now as individuals, and not assume that just because I look good in a tux they are all longing for me to fall for them.'

'It's Dempsey you must thank,' she told him. 'He's a great guy. He jogged your conscience, not me. I'm not sure that he ought to have done it either. I wanted to forget it.'

'He was mad at me—real mad! Just like a Western hero in the films.' Zendik smiled at the memory. 'All he needed was a white horse. Miranda, I'm not making fun of him. I admire him very much.'

'So do I.' Jake was probably the only one she would miss when she went down to KL to work.

They reached, and passed, the cable car station, the tiny car looking like a toy in the sky. The road got steeper as it wound round in tighter circles. Miranda lapsed into a daydream, remembering everything that had happened that day she and Bill had first made that perilous journey. The first day she had met Jon. . . And for a moment she remembered the poison in the lovely eyes of Mary Ann Moon—and wondered if she had known of the side-effects of that quinine she had given her.

'I won't expect you to come and hear me again,' said Zendik, 'but I'm glad we made peace, Miranda. And I mean it—about not forgetting you when I travel around the world.'

Miranda was jerked back from her memories back into Zendik's cushy limousine. She felt a foot taller now, calm and completely recovered from her dreadful depression. She held out her hand, and Zen took it with a firm grip. 'All over now. Good luck, Zen.'

'Good luck to you. And God bless you.' She was slightly surprised to hear a Hindu give her a blessing. But then she was pleased. He reverenced the same God her father did.

She was glad that they were friends again. She would leave Genting without any dark areas that she dared not remember.

She almost jumped out of the car, pulling her bag with her. She felt light-hearted and well, even better than she had when she first came. She carried herself calmer now, older and wiser and less impressionable. It was a good feeling.

Singh was there, all six foot three of him, in his glittering turban. He greeted her with a *namaste,* putting both hands together before reaching for her bag. 'I'll see it goes up. How are you, little memsahib?'

'I'm fine. Are you?'

'We heard you had the serious illness. It was said that you were dying.' He smiled a wide white smile. 'But I see from your lightness of foot that there is nothing left of any illness.'

Miranda thought first she would go in search of Bill, but then common sense reminded her that she had just come out of hospital, and that she ought to lie down for a while. So she hung up her dresses and lay back on her bed, glad that one bad phase of her life was over, looking forward with eagerness to the next one.

She went down to Suzy's that night knowing herself fully. She knew why she had not enjoyed the job here. She was the vicar's daughter, who felt guilty when she was idle. But it was different now. She was on a brief holiday before she went down the mountain for good. She would enjoy Genting as a holiday, and for the first time really appreciate its beauty, its pleasures and its luxury. Suzy had seen her coming, and the Empress special was on their table. The others weren't there yet. Miranda chatted for a while to Suzy, who also thought she had been at death's door.

'Princess!' Jake had just spotted her. She jumped up and ran to meet him, and they hugged each other wordlessly, then they walked back to the table with arms around each other. There were tears in Jake's eyes that he didn't bother to wipe away. He said chokily, 'You need someone to look after you, girl.'

'I'm going to have someone,' she told him.' I'm going to work for Jonathan Smith.'

'You serious? That's good, kid. You were restless here.'

Miranda smiled at him affectionately. 'How come you know me so well, Dempsey?'

'Jest lived a whole lot longer, kid.' His eyes were keen as he looked at her. 'See much of Jonathan, did you?'

'He looked after me.'

'I thought he might.'

Then it was Bill's turn to look delighted. 'You made it! I missed you, Miranda. Have you told your parents yet? I was worried sick in case I had to write to them.' He came round and gave her a hug too.

'Your looking very prosperous, Bill,' Miranda smiled.

'That's the name of the game,' he grinned, and looked very relieved to see her. 'Another drink? The usual?'

'Better not, thanks. My liver is still a bit fragile.' She sat back in her chair. 'Tell me all the latest gossip. What's been going on while I've been otherwise engaged? Has Isabel been gentle with you?'

Bill was enthusiastic about Isabel da Costa. 'She's a financial wizard, that woman. She's Heng's equal, that's for sure. She's on the Board, and he takes her advice about every move.'

Jake said lazily, 'Except one.'

'Oh yes, that one.' Bill was grinning as he turned again to Miranda. 'Heng's latest lady friend is Dr Moon. They've been almost inseparable lately.'

'And she's come into one or two interesting little diamonds.'

'Not engaged?' Miranda was laughing with them.

'No. A diamond necklace, wasn't it, Bill?'

'That's right, and matching earrings. No wonder he's glad of Isabel's expert advice on investments. I wonder what old Kim will think of Moon as a step-mother?'

They were all laughing as Maidie joined them, her fingers outstretched because her nails weren't dry. 'Hi, honey. You feelin' better? These guys were all off their food when we heard.'

'How's the wrist?'

Maidie held it out for Miranda's attention. 'Healed well. Those scars will fade, Maidie,' Miranda assured her.

'I don't care if they don't. I'm through putting appearances first.'

Miranda smiled, 'For someone who says that, you're looking remarkably pretty today!'

'Hear, hear.' Bill was approving. And Miranda could tell that his infatuation with the lovely little American had ripened into true friendship. So Bill too was growing up. Their spell on the mountaintop was doing them both good, however painful it had been on the way.

As they went through to the Blue Lagoon together, slowly and with a lot of joking laughter, Miranda told Bill about her decision to go and work at Jonathan's Klinik. 'And don't read romance into it, Bill. I just want to do more of a job. Will you explain to Heng, or shall I?'

'I'll do it. He won't mind. As I said, Isabel's doing two jobs, so she's happy. And she's useful to Heng, so he's happy with the way things are.' He smiled at her. 'And I expect we'll see you for the odd weekend, so I'm happy.' Miranda looked relieved. 'But considering the way you first met, I'm afraid I won't believe that it's nothing at all to do with your future boss's handsome face and neat way with the chatting up bit.'

'He doesn't do that when he's working. It's only a way of relaxing.'

'Mmm.' Bill led the way into the Blue Lagoon, and Miranda looked around her, happy to be back. He went on, speaking into her ear as he pulled out her chair for her, 'We'll just see who he brings up next time he relaxes, then.' And she ignored that question, knowing that she was just as interested as he in the answer.

Next morning, Miranda decided that she ought to see Mr Heng herself. It wasn't Bill's job to resign for her. With

her new-found confidence, she explained simply and sen-
sibly why she had made up her mind to go. Mr Heng
nodded, and agreed that things were going smoothly with
Isabel Da Costa as Sister, and he had no objection to
Miranda leaving if she wanted another job. 'But if it is only
lack of employment, why not ask Dr Moon if you could
work at the hospital here?' he queried.

'I never thought of it.' Miranda went across to the hospital. If she were genuine about wanting more work, she
should seek it here first. She knew at the back of her mind
that it was Jonathan she really wanted, but she allowed
herself to be deceived, and asked to speak to Dr Moon.

Mary Ann Moon was curt and dismissive. 'I'm sorry,
but no, there is no place here.'

'I thought you were short-staffed,' Miranda remarked.

'We don't need anyone permanent.'

'But—'

'If this eagerness for work is because Jonathan Smith
thinks you are a flighty kid, then forget it.'

'He couldn't—' Miranda began.

'Oh yes, he did.' Mary Ann seemed to take pleasure in
repeating it. 'He once said you would never find a real
nurse taking a job at the Empress.'

Miranda realised she would get nowhere with Mary
Ann, so she smiled, thanked her politely, and left. She had
maintained her dignity with Moon—but oh dear, did Jonathan really see her as a flighty kid? She would have to
work very hard to dispel that image. It was a good thing
she had been told; now she knew where she was in the surgeon's estimation. She walked back slowly, among the
wedding-like abundance of cherry blossom that fell from
the trees like confetti. Jonathan had never made her feel
small when they had talked, but now she realised that his
attitude to her was protective rather than romantic. He did
see her as a juvenile. She was annoyed, but glad too that
she knew. It would make it more fun, showing him the
woman she really was.

She was touched by Heng's concern about her welfare. 'Let me know where you will stay, and I will make sure Kim calls on you.' He wrote out a cheque for the pay that was due.

'The nurses' home at the Klinik,' Miranda told him.

'Good. That is a reasonable area. She will be all right, Bill.' Mr Heng had developed more humanity, being in love. She smiled and thanked him. It was only later when she looked at the cheque that she saw how generous he had been, considering that she had done so little work.

She phoned the Klinik that evening. Yes, she could start whenever she wished. Mr Smith had expected her to take a week off to recuperate, he had told Sister Leonie. He himself would be going away in a couple of days. Yes, abroad. There was a symposium in London, and he usually took his time getting back. Miranda decided then and there that she would start in two days. She might be going to the Devereux Klinik only to work, but she wasn't going to miss seeing Jon if he was planning to be away for some time.

'Two days?' Jake was the first person she told. 'Honey, it's your life. But we sure better make the most of today. How about a picnic—the four of us? First thing tomorrow. The weather forecast is fine. And if you're to be ward-bashing in two days' time, you need a spot of genuine idleness.'

Miranda saw Cherry too, that night. 'Don't break your heart, Miranda,' Cherry advised. 'It is only you that thinks you are going there to look after patients.'

'I'm not going after Jonathan Smith. He's way out of my class—and age group,' Miranda protested.

'Well, don't forget our house. Mama will be happy to see you any time.'

'I'm not going to get hurt, Cherry. But thanks.'

She hoped nobody else thought what Cherry thought. Her humiliation with Zendik was public enough. Surely no one would think for a minute that her change of job was because of Jonathan?

Bill had taken the morning off, to go on the picnic with Miranda. Maidie was up too, though she often slept till noon. 'This is fun,' she laughed. 'Miranda, go and tell Jake to bring his guitar. We'll go on the Lake. It's always nice with music.'

Jake was just up. 'Hi.' His eyes were bleary and he hadn't combed his hair or beard. 'I'm ready. Didn't sleep much.' He rubbed his eyes and buttoned his shirt, tucking it into his jeans. 'Goin' to give you a real fine send-off.'

'Maidie said to bring the guitar,' Miranda told him.

He nodded. When he was ready, they walked along the corridor together. She felt as though she had known him for a hundred years. As they stood waiting for the lift, he said, 'I met you here. I knew you was a princess right from the start.'

'You make it sound sad, Jake. I'm only going down to the city. I'll be back.'

'Sure.' He hoisted the guitar more safely on to his back, and Miranda watched him, concerned. He looked down at her and smiled. 'Okay, kid?'

'I'm okay, Dempsey.'

Just before they met the others he stopped. 'Hey, English princess! How did you ever think of leaving your vicarage to cross half the world?'

'To learn about it, Jake,' Miranda told him.

'Have you learned?'

She knew what he was asking. 'Yes, my old friend. Thanks to you I have, and it didn't hurt a bit.'

His face brightened, and he put his arm loosely about her shoulders as they went up to the other two, who stood in the sunshine together. 'That's all I wanted to hear, pardner!' he grinned.

They set off, walking to the lake because it was such a lovely day. The sound of horses made them move to one side. Miranda knew who would be astride the leading bay. This time Zendik reined in, turned the horse to come back to talk to them. 'How are you? Why don't you join us?'

His pretty companion waited a few feet away, the horse proud and stately as it stamped and puffed.

Jake turned to Miranda. 'Want to?'

She smiled up at Zendik, relaxed with him. 'We're going on a picnic,' she told them. And the singer looked down into her eyes rather longer than was decent, before he reined in the horse and clapped his heels to his sides. The two were soon hidden by the willows along the bank.

Jake said, 'You could have gone.'

Miranda laughed. 'With the Mogul emperor? No, thanks.' And she moved closer to him to say quietly, 'And thanks for making him apologise. He didn't mean any harm.'

'Glad it's sorted out. It was a helluva way to grow up.'

They pushed out one of the boats. It was very quiet, with only the lapping of the water, and the cries of children along the bank. Jake was very critical of Bill's rowing style. 'The idea is to move the water, brother, not wet the guitar!' The sun was warm on their faces. The men took off their shirts. The very quietness soothed them all, lulled their senses. Then Jake sang, and Bill rested on his oars to listen. Jake pointed to a canvas bag. 'Help yourselves.' It was a bottle of wine and four glasses. They drank and sang, and talked more freely, tongues loosened by the wine.

Through they met again in the evening, it was the picnic that Miranda remembered, when she was miles away. Sometimes it brought tears to her eyes. They had had some good times, special times. She hoped that Jake and Maidie would be happy.

It was quite late next day when she reported for duty at Jon's Klinik. She had decided to pack all her things, leave nothing behind at the Empress, even though she knew she would be back there before returning to England. She refused any company and took an ordinary taxi down the mountain. The hospital was in darkness. Perhaps she ought to go straight to the nurses' home.

But then she saw a light in the outpatients' section, and knocked on the door there. No one answered. She opened the door and looked in—perhaps the cleaners were in.

She peeped in, making no sound. Jonathan Smith was sitting at his desk, going through a pile of papers. Miranda watched him for a few moments, admiring the way he looked, the way he worked.

Then there were footsteps behind her, and Miranda turned quickly. It was a delivery boy, with a cardboard box. Jonathan looked up. 'Is that you, Chin?' He stood up. 'Good to see you. I'm getting hungry.' Then he saw Miranda standing in the shadows.

The boy handed over the food and Jon watched him go, then he smiled at Miranda. 'Come in, please. Chin always cooks enough for two.'

'I'm sorry—I didn't come deliberately to see you,' she explained. 'I know how busy you are. But I saw a light. I'll go over to the nurses' home.'

'Be quiet, and come in.'

Miranda obeyed. She could not pretend. Inside herself she was exultant that she had at least seen him before his overseas trip. The two of them faced each other, and she felt so happy that she forgot she ought to be respectful. 'It's good to be able to report for duty to the head man,' she told him.

'It is indeed.' Jon stood up, stretched his arms and back. 'Now there are plates and forks in that cupboard. I often don't go home at all when I'm busy. Help yourself while I put these things away.' He took off his white coat. He wore a thin short-sleeved shirt over grey slacks, and Miranda stole a quick glance at his physical perfection as she took the things from the cupboard. She opened the box, which contained indeed enough fried rice for two, if not three, and spooned it out. 'Thank you—good girl! Now let's have a chat before I go away. You really think you're going to like it here?'

She wished he hadn't called her a good girl; it reminded her rather strongly of what Mary Ann had said—that he regarded her as a flighty little thing. She said coolly, 'Yes, so long as there's plenty to do.'

'There is. Mr Radakrishnan will be taking over from me as chief. Surgery will go on as usual, so you'll be kept very busy.' His eyes were twinkling as he ate his rice and watched her sideways. She had the feeling that he was making fun of her.

'Have you thought any more of having a prevention department?' she asked. 'Teach patients to eat properly, take exercise, avoid stress? We did talk of it once.' She was determined to sound businesslike.

Jonathan smiled. 'I have thought of it, but had no time to do anything about it, Miranda. While I'm away, maybe you'd work on the idea for me? Rasa Khalid is my chief physio, she's a treasure. Chat to her about the scheme, and have something on paper for me when I get back.'

Miranda glowed with delight. Something to work on, an opportunity to show Mr Devereux-Smith that she had something inside her head, that she was no longer the simple little creature who saw trolls and dragons in the mountain caves. 'I'd like that. You won't want to take on extra staff? Use the existing physio department?'

'An exra physio won't break the bank. But see how you get on in theory first. It's a damn good idea, but I'm chary about taking any more on my plate personally. Being a bachelor means that I work far too hard, I'm afraid. I often sleep here to save the bother of driving home.'

Miranda said firmly, 'Then I'll bear that in mind. We could make sure the health promotion only takes place when you're operating, so you wouldn't get involved.'

'Right. Now that's arranged, tell me, how are your friends up at Genting? They must have been sorry you didn't stay longer with them.'

'They understood. And it isn't all that far away.'

'You're a friend of the famous Zendik, I understand. He's a nice enough chap, isn't he? Not many brains, but masses of personality.' Jon was dismissive of Zendik. And Miranda felt her face growing pink at the realisation that Jon had been told of her indiscretion by the ever watchful Mary Ann.

'We're on speaking terms.' She tried to make light of the relationship, then took the initiative away from him by asking, 'When will your next trip be?'

'Not for quite a while. When I get back from UK I'll put in a good long stint here.' He smiled at her. 'Don't get the idea that I'm a playboy. I only go away when I feel I need a break.'

'I understand that. I never thought you were a playboy at all. But I think you believe that of me, when it isn't true at all.'

Jon said softly, 'I never judge people until I know them. I don't think I know you yet, Miranda. But I do hope I will. It's such fun finding out.'

She had softened at his tone, and now met his smile with her own. 'You're so very good at saying the appropriate thing. I wish I could. I always think of something nice to say when I'm by myself. Never at the time.'

'Then I'll be around to find out if you have anything nice to say about me.' Jon stood up to take the plates away. As he came back, he put his hand on her shoulder. 'I really hope you can.'

'I'll try.' Miranda stood up too. 'Thank you very much for supper. Can I—?'

'No, you can't help me at all. Off you go to the nurses' home, get a good night's sleep. It isn't an easy job, and you haven't really taken enough time for convalescence, you know. So take life gently while I'm away.' He walked to the door with her. 'And please try to find something nice to say to me when I come back. I'll be looking forward to it.'

She looked up at him. It seemed so sad to say goodbye just as she had met him again. Suddenly he bent and kissed her cheek very quickly. She turned then and walked away. He would not want anyone to see him being familiar with the new nurse. But her heart was fluttering in a very gratified way at the endearment, as she opened the door of the house across the garden, and looked around for anyone to show her where to sleep.

She had a small but neat pretty room on the ground floor. She decided to take Jon's advice and get some sleep. She was both tired and excited by the day. And by the challenge he had given her—to make definite plans for a healthy persons' clinic. She lay on the single bed, simple and not as luxurious as the one in Genting, looking up at the fan as it wafted air over her body. She wore the thinnest of cotton nightdresses, but her illness had acclimatised her to the heat now, and she stood it well.

She was happy. She was as close to Jonathan as she could be. She had the chance of proving to him that she had something inside her head. Miranda sighed. Yes, of course she was happy to be here rather than at Genting, yet the happier she was, the harder it would be to go home. Four months of her year were almost gone. At first the year had stretched interminably; now it seemed all too soon that she would have to leave. Ah well, she would make the most of what she had. She would always remember Jonathan, wherever she went in the world. He was very special. From the very first day, he had been the most important part of her Malaysian stay. Miranda slept with that calming thought in her mind.

CHAPTER NINE

MIRANDA thought she would feel deflated, knowing that Jonathan was not at the Klinik. But as she woke on her first day as Sister on Surgical Ward Two, the sun filled her room with brightness, and she could hear the bustling of the morning rush hour outside the nurses' home. It was thrilling. Life was going to be a challenge. And she was determined to work well, and make life here a success.

Sister Leonie she had already met. She was tall and lissom, half Australian, with sun-bleached hair swept into a chignon, tanned handsome face, and a good head for administration. 'You sure you don't mind being put on Surgical?' She was willing to be flexible. 'It's pretty hard going, and you haven't been long back on your feet after your hepatitis.'

'I'll do anything. I feel great.' Miranda had been easy-going and willing.

'Well, Mr Radakrishnan is operating, so you'll be best to stay on S2. As you get used to the routine, I'll leave it more in your hands.'

The post-op routine was the same in any hospital. Beds had to be prepared, drips available, oxygen connected. It was good to be busy, and Miranda was still working when it was time to go for lunch. Instead of taking food from the local Malay café, she bought some bread, and took a sandwich and a papaya into the gardens. The others told her it was too hot, but she was fascinated by the different trees and flowers, by the vivid birds and the constantly changing city sounds.

Then she found out what they meant. It was time to go back to the ward, and she found herself hot and sticky. No wonder there were three clean overalls provided! It was necessary to change before going back on duty. The afternoon was less hectic, as most patients only wanted to sleep, and had to be monitored hourly or four-hourly. Miranda happily carried this out herself instead of delegating to the nurses, for which they were grateful. Any initial shyness was soon dissipated, as soon as they found that the new English Sister was gentle and soft-spoken, willing to work with them, and anxious to learn.

She got to know the names of the patients as soon as she could; she knew they appreciated it. And she took a look at the list on Surgical One—only to see that a Mr Suk was there, operated on by Mr Smith two days ago. She asked Sister Leonie if she could see him. It was indeed the same man. He beamed with delight when he saw her.

'Of course I am well. Mr Smith very good surgeon. I come to his Klinik straight from Empress.' He held out a hand and took hers. 'But maybe I would not be here at all, if you did not come to me so quickly when I have my heart attack.'

'I remember,' said Miranda. 'It was my first day. We went to the Orchid Room because Jake and Maidie were singing.'

'It was the little Maidie singing that start my trouble.' He laughed heartily, holding his breastbone with both hands. 'They tell me this bone take three months to heal, but I cannot stay solemn all that time. I love to laugh.'

'That's a good thing. It's good to see you so well.' She turned to go.

'Sister Mason.' His voice was serious now. 'I have you to thank for my life.'

'Mr Smith saved your life,' Miranda corrected.

'You did as much as he.' When she did not answer, he said, 'So you are shy to be the hero? Then I will speak of it no more. But in my heart I will not forget you.'

She was touched. 'Don't give your heart too much to do,' she cautioned.

'Such memories make it stronger.'

It was gratifying to have such a start to her work here. When it was time to go off duty, Miranda was exhausted. She had forgotten she was not over the effects of her illness. Still, she had made her choice, and she was happy to have had such a wonderful day. She lay on her bed, too tired to undress, and watched the fan rotate through her yawns. What a sensible choice she had made, to come here, to leave Genting with its unhappy reminders of unsatisfactory work, of the unkindness of Mary Ann, and the constant sight of Zendik. Yes, she was going to enjoy working in the big city. Perhaps tomorrow she would meet the physio, Rasa Khalid, and they could begin to plan the new department.

The phone rang. She had slipped into sleep, and thought she was dreaming its shrill notes. But when it did not stop, she reached out and lifted the receiver, her eyes still closed. 'Hello?'

'Miranda, you sound tired out. Are you all right?'

'Hello, Bill. How nice of you to ring. I've had a glorious day.'

'You sound washed up.'

'It was a bit tiring,' she admitted.

'Are you sure you should be working full-time?'

Miranda had woken up now, and sat up leaning on one elbow. 'Of course. I love it here. I'll soon get into the swing of things.'

'Is Smith there?'

'No—gone to London.'

'And you still like it?'

Exasperated, she said, 'Bill, now do you believe me? I came for the work, not the boss.'

'I'll try and believe you,' he teased. 'The others wouldn't come and eat until they heard how you were.'

'That's sweet. Give them my love. And tell Maidie that Mr Suk has had his coronary bypass op. He says he still loves to laugh, and intends to come and see her again when he's out of here.'

They parted in good humour. Miranda was over her tiredness after that, and felt warm and content that she had such good friends. Bill faithfully rang every evening for the first week. Maidie then decided that she would come down to do some shopping, and the four of them spent Saturday wandering around the local shops, the girls trying on everything from saris to sarongs. They went for lunch to a small Kentucky Fried Chicken House—Jake insisted that the waitresses wouldn't even know where Kentucky was, and that the chicken would taste awful. But it was tasty, and they were glad to sit down and drink cold beer.

Someone passed them on the way out. 'Hello, Miranda.'

It was Sister Leonie, looking glamorous in a slinky Malay dress and trousers, her head covered as so many locals did. Bill was impressed, and suggested that they come back with her to see the place where she lived.

'Sister Leonie doesn't sleep in,' smiled Miranda.

'All the same, I'll bring some flowers for Mr Suk.' Maidie was curious to see the famous Devereux Klinik.

So before they went back to Genting, the threesome came back with Miranda and made sure she was comfortable. 'I can't take every weekend off,' she warned.

'Okay, workaholic, if that's the way you feel,' teased Jake.

'I do have some work to do. A bit of reorganisation.' She didn't want to speak too much about her idea, but she had begun to make lists of what she might need, and was waiting for a chance to talk in detail to Rasa Khalid, who was quite keen on the idea.

Maidie came back from visiting Mr Suk. 'He's cute. I'm so glad he's going to be okay.' She took a parcel from her shopping basket. 'Here, Miranda, this is for you. I see you have a pool in the hospital grounds. Use it.'

When they had gone, Miranda unwrapped the parcel. It was an elegant batik *pareo*, a wrap to go over her black and white bikini. That was sweet of Maidie. She hadn't been swimming yet, but the pool was just close to the nurses' home, and quite private.

But her work, plus the job of organising her department—she and Rasa had begun to call it the Good Health Club—made it hard to find spare time. By the time she got back at nights, she was glad to sleep a good healthy sleep. They had decided that the physio department itself would be the basis of the club. Leaflets had to be written, with advice about diet, about exercise, about posture, fresh air—all in the several languages of the capital—English, Malay, Tamil and Chinese. They had decided also that regular sessions kept people on their toes; if they only attended when they felt like it, it was easy to slip into bad habits. By the time Jonathan was expected back, Miranda had all the paper work he could possibly ask for—except the amount they should charge annually for membership.

But Jonathan did not return at the end of three weeks, and news filtered through that he had taken a skiing holiday in Switzerland. Miranda decided that he must have met someone interesting, and was in no hurry to get back. She had no claim over him, after all. And she was busy enough not to feel anything but slightly disappointed at not being able to present her wonderful ideas to him when they were ready. She put the sheaf of papers in her drawer, and took no further interest in her notes.

Rasa Khalid, however, had become keen. She was a dark-skinned girl, rather thin and very athletic. She could bend her wiry body into all the positions of yoga, and her mind was as mobile as her body. She and Miranda had become quite friendly, finding that they were both quiet and modest people, with similar tastes in clothes and music.

'I would like to invite you to our home, Miranda. It is Deepavali next week. I hope you are off duty.' Miranda was, but queried the name.

'Deepavali? Our main festival of the year. All Hindus celebrate. We go to the temple, and light candles in our homes. Some decorate their homes with garlands, and we eat and drink and entertain all our friends.'

Miranda was very pleased to be asked. 'Your parents don't mind? That I'm a Christian?'

'They like me to take you. I want to go to Batu Road one lunch hour to buy some new clothes—we always like to wear something new. Will you come with me?'

'Love to. I went to Batu Road with my friend from Genting. You'll be wearing a sari?' Miranda asked. 'I've always seen you in Western clothes.'

'Naturally. But I will not expect you to go to the Temple. I will meet you later. And bring your notes about the Club, we can discuss our plans further.'

And so yet another week passed, with spare time spent choosing a new outfit each, and yet more talk about the proposed new club. Miranda had got over the weariness of her illness, but she still led such a busy life that when she went to bed at night, she fell straight to sleep. Bill telephoned less frequently now, convinced that all was well with her.

Deepavali was a spectacular festival. There were street processions, with dancers carrying lighted candles, with so much gold and silver jewellery and glittering embroidery around the hems of saris and dresses that the night sky's allowance of stars seemed to have doubled. Afterwards, the table in the Khalids' home in the suburbs was laden with dishes, savoury and spicy. Miranda was welcomed warmly, and encouraged to try everything, which she did to the best of her ability.

'Would you like to drive to the Batu caves?' It was Rasa's older brother who offered. 'They are beautiful at this time, ablaze with colour.'

Miranda was keen. 'I may never see them again,' she realised.

'There are hundreds of steps.'

She laughed. 'Then I'll watch you climb them!'

So Rajendra drove the girls out to the caves. There seemed to be thousands of people, in the gayest and most colourful garments. Miranda elected to wait by the car, while Rasa and her brother made efforts to snake through the crowds to get to the front. The people were climbing the steep steps, a moving mass of humanity up the side of the cliff.

A voice in the crowd seemed to say her name. But it was dark, and there were too many people around her. She was not very tall. However, in a moment, he was at her side—the great Zendik himself, with Hassan. 'It is so nice to meet you here,' he smiled. 'You celebrate Deepavali too?'

'With my friends. How are you, Zendik? Hassan?'

Hassan said, 'It is this guy—so religious he is these days! Even if it means going on late, he insisted we drive down here.'

Miranda looked into Zendik's face. The dark eyes were shining with a sort of honesty. She said, 'I think it's wonderful to come and celebrate the triumph of good over evil.'

The great man nodded eagerly. 'Exactly. You see, Hassan, I may be only a coathanger dressed up, but even I can comprehend that.' And Miranda felt uncomfortable, remembering Jon's words—Not many brains but plenty of personality. . .

She said warmly, 'I'm really glad we met.'

He said, '*Namaste*.' And then they were swallowed up in the crush.

Rajendra drove her back to the nurses' home. It was very late, but her heart was overflowing with happiness and excitement. She was far too preoccupied to notice the single light burning in the Devereux Klinik, as she ran up the steps of the home, and straight to her bed, still carrying a silver balloon that someone had handed her in the crowd.

Next morning the pool was deserted as usual. Miranda looked out of her window, and decided that she could no longer resist the flickering shadows of the trees around the water, the twinkling sunlight as it filtered through, the breeze warm and friendly, making the water dance.

She put on her bikini and wrapped herself in the matching *pareo* that Maidie had bought her. The sky was luminous with the sunrise, as splashes of rainbow colours lit the cloudless blue. Miranda slipped into the water quietly, and rolled over on her back, so that she could see the sunrise as she swam. The water was delicious. Wrapped in its tender softness, she swam lazily around the pool, letting her hair float free behind her. Why had she not done this much earlier? She was physically and mentally completely relaxed. And she had surely earned this sensual delight, by her long week of devotion to her patients. She turned over and over like a slim young dolphin. She would stay here for hours, or as long as the colours in the sky were changing so wonderfully. She looked at it through the fingers of the palm leaves. They reminded her of the fingernails of Siamese dancers, artificially elongated to make them more elegant and evocative.

'Miranda!'

She heard her name, but thought she had imagined it. The sparrows were chirping loudly, and her ears were under the water. The distant rumble of rush hour was muffled. It was easy to hear things that weren't there. . .

'Miranda!' She rolled over to look idly at the pool edge, where the frangipani bushes were shedding their white stars heady with fragrance. There was someone there, and his tall figure was quite unmistakable. Jonathan. And she felt a total physical reaction, as though her whole body reacted at seeing him so near. She allowed her feet to touch the floor, shook back her soaking hair.

'Hello, Jon.'

He didn't reply at once, but bent down slowly on to one knee to see her more clearly. Her heart raced, but she maintained her calm exterior. She must be adult about this. Of course she was infatuated with the handsome surgeon. They were almost friends. But it was nothing more. It would pass. He had a string of women, all more sophisticated and elegant than she, able to speak his language.

'Have you breakfasted?' he asked.

'No, I came straight here. The water was just irresistible.'

He swallowed. 'I know what you mean.'

Miranda gazed up into his well-loved face, the sun emphasising his cheekbones. Had he lost a little weight? It was hard to see the blue of his eyes in the bright sunlight. They were hooded, unreadable. But were they? She recognised a fire in them and saw that he was watching her pale body in the rippling water. She knew she was causing a similar physical reaction in him to that she herself felt.

Suddenly embarrassed, she stood up straight and reached for her *pareo*. Jon reached it first, and held it while she selfconsciously climbed out of the water. He handed it to her, and she wrapped it round her under her arms.

He said, 'You shared my last meal here. How about breakfast?'

Miranda looked up. He seemed even taller when she was wearing no shoes. Oh, how pleased she was that he was here again! And yet—the rumours of his affair in Switzerland reminded her not to be naïveany more about men, least of all such a knowledgeable one as Jonathan Smith. 'I would like breakfast. I'll try to be quick.'

'Yes, do—I'm hungry. I'll be in the car.'

'All right.'

Miranda walked quickly indoors, knowing that if she ran she might fall and look silly. She hastily washed the chlorine from her body, towelled briskly, and put on her peacock blue shift—loose and comfortable in the sticky heat that was beginning to build up. Her hair was almost dry in the heat. She only need brush it hard, and find her sandals, and she was ready. Conscious of the increased beat of her heart, she made her way, outwardly calm, to the car park.

She knew which car was his. It had been kept under cover while he was away—a new dark green Rover. Typical of him, to have a wildly expensive vehicle—all imported cars had huge duty to pay on them. He might even be a millionaire—top surgeons could name their price. And here was she, invited to share breakfast with a millionaire. She smiled at herself. No, Jon Smith was too modest a man to charge the earth. Status meant little to him, or else he would use his full name, flaunt his money. It was the likes of Zendik who did that.

'That was quick, Miranda. Thanks,' smiled Jon.

'Thank you for asking me.'

He opened the door for her, went round and got in himself. 'You sound like a little girl on a Sunday school picnic!' he teased. He started the engine and eased the car out into the busy traffic.

Miranda wasn't sure whether to take offence or not. However, it did make it clear that he still thought of her as a child. His attentions, as she had told herself a dozen times, were protective, and not romantic. She looked across at him as he concentrated on the three lanes of traffic. 'Then by all means think of me as one,' she said. There, let him find out. He would soon know that she had made a success of her work, that she had done all the planning for the club that he had entrusted to her. Then she would see if he still called her a little girl. . . 'Where are we going?' she asked.

'Peninsula Court, my place in Thambi Dollah.' He smiled at her. 'And no, I won't be cooking. They're service apartments. We have a good pool too, you must come up and swim with me.'

'Thambi Dollah isn't far.'

'No. And breakfast is already ordered. You must be hungry after all that swimming.'

'How long were you watching me?' She felt her cheeks grow warm.

'About half an hour—or was it an hour? Forgive me, I don't usually intrude on the private life of my staff, but you looked so very pretty, and you enjoyed it so very much.'

They had arrived at a large wrought iron gate. Jonathan had no need to sound his horn. An armed guard in pseudo-military combat jacket and boots snapped smartly to attention before running to unlock the padlock. The gates swung wide and they swept along a drive flanked by bougainvillea bushes, luxuriously growing all down the sides, their purple blossoms vivid and lovely. The pool was next, white marble-tiled, and also guarded by a burly man, who was supervising the attempts of a tiny Chinese boy to dog-paddle his way across.

'It's lovely!' exlaimed Miranda.

'I know. I don't know why I don't spend more time here,' said Jon.

There was yet another armed man waiting impassively to take them up in the lift. Jon said as they zoomed skyward, 'It isn't Alcatraz—only looks like it from the outside. The residents believe in peace of mind, and don't mind paying for it. Thanks, Hamid.'

At the door of the penthouse, Jon took out his key and slipped off his shoes, Oriental fashion. Miranda did the same. She had become used to it since being in KL Jon then led the way into a magnificent apartment, with a picture window looking out across miles of city to the far cliffs. 'Make yourself comfortable. I'll just open the champagne,' he said.

She looked at him in astonishment, and he laughed. 'You've heard of a champagne breakfast?'

'Well, yes.'

'I want to celebrate being back. It's good. And it seems daft to celebrate alone. You are glad to see me back, aren't you, Miranda?'

She accepted the champagne, in a tall smooth glass. She looked up at him from the long grey velvet sofa in front of the panoramic view of the city, and knew she was no longer in awe of him. It was a superb, thrilling discovery. She smiled at him and said openly, 'Oh yes, Jon, I'm very glad you're back where you belong. We missed you.'

He sat next to her. 'I missed *you*.'

'But the symposium was a success?'

'The whole trip was successful. Very satisfactory indeed.' He had no time to say more, as the breakfast arrived on a low trolley, ready to serve. It was traditional English ham and eggs with mushrooms, fruit, toast and a large silver pot of coffee.

'This is superb.' Miranda realised how hungry she was after all that swimming. 'I didn't think I'd eat again after the Deepavali feast last night.'

'You have a busy social life, then?' He handed her a delicate china plate of ham and eggs.

'Amazingly busy.' She didn't see his slight frown as he helped himself from the hotplate. Just then the phone rang, and he excused himself. She heard him answer it in the hall. 'Yes, great time. Late? Oh, affair of the heart.'

CHAPTER TEN

MIRANDA took a deep breath. She wouldn't call it a gasp, because it was common knowledge among the gossips of the Devereux Klinik that Jon Smith liked a good time. But now that she had heard it from his own lips, it would be even easier to accept his attention as that of a bachelor with many strings to his bow and no intention of settling for one girl when he could have many. 'An affair of the heart'—that was a tactful way of putting it. He probably meant an affair of the body. And she blushed at her own thoughts, and bent over her breakfast.

Jon came back. She said lightly, 'This is delicious.'

'Good. Let's hope no one else phones to welcome me home. That was Radakrishnan, by the way—says you got on well without me.'

'We did. No problems. I say, it was nice to meet Mr Suk—still as cheerful as ever. There's a good atmosphere in your Klinik, Mr Smith. I think that must reflect the character of the man at the top.'

'Thanks for that.' They chatted easily, reminding Miranda of their first night, when he had stayed with her nearly all night. But this time she felt more equal. And she certainly knew that he would not be interested in her as a woman. She was not the glamorous type he went for. He said casually, 'So you've seen Zendik again?'

'Oh yes, we met yesterday. I remembered what you said about no brains and lots of personality.' She saw him wince.

'Did I say that? Miranda, I'm occasionally a heel, but I swear I don't mean it.'

She laughed. 'Shall I pour you another cup of coffee? I ought to tell you what Jake Dempsey said about you.'

'I don't think I want to hear.' He held out his cup, relaxed and smiling.

Miranda tried to imitate Jake's accent. 'Waal, comes up a coupla times a year to relax—drinks some wine, plays some blackjack, brings a different woman each time—knows how to wind down, does Mr Smith.'

Jon leaned back with his cup in his hands, laughing at her accent. 'I guess you must be the next Mrs Siddons!'

'I hope not, Jon. Her speciality was tragedy.'

'Of course. I say, Miranda, didn't you feel a little bit homesick when you knew I was going to England?'

'A little.' Her homesickness had come a bit earlier.

'Those winding lanes of Berkshire, the stream running past your garden, the apple tree in the back garden laden with fruit—'

'How did you know that?'

'You told me—that first night we talked, remember?' She nodded slowly. She had told him about home, but had she gone into such detail? She was quite a raw conversationalist at that time.

She shook her head, and pushed away her cup. 'I'm too busy enjoying being here to be homesick. There's lots of time for nostalgia when I have to go back.'

'So you do like it here?'

'Oh, very much. I'm so grateful you let me come here and do some proper work. When can I tell you about the good health club we've planned?'

'Tomorrow,' he said firmly. 'Today is Sunday and I'm having a day of rest. Where shall we have lunch?'

'After that breakfast?' Miranda spoke lightly, but she knew she didn't want to leave him yet. They were so easy together, so very right, in spite of their differences, and his affairs of the heart. She stole another look at him, and he turned and smiled, intimately, slowly, his eyes following the lines of her face. He put back a stray strand of her hair with gentle fingers, and she tried not to shiver with pleasure at the touch. She spoke without even thinking that her question might be impertinent. 'Jon, how can a man like you not be married?'

'I'm not sure.' He looked down then, his blue eyes unreadable, and she sensed she had touched on something she ought not to. 'Give me a while and I'll answer that one. But after all, I have many admirers. Money is no problem, nor is status. I'm accepted in aristocratic homes, revered by all my patients and *some* of my staff, and my fame has spread over most of South-East Asia.' He was smiling now. 'Do you still pity me, Miranda?'

'I didn't say I did.' What she had actually thought was how come the best-looking man in the world was still single. 'But would you like a family one day?'

'Naturally.' The attendant came up to take the trolley away then. When he had gone, neither of them took up that subject. Miranda wondered if she ought to go, but Jon was clearly enjoying their chat. She said, 'Tell me more about London.'

'Hmm. There's a heck of a lot going on there just now. I think I ought to go back at least once a year or two. Transplants isn't really my field, though I've done two and one is still alive, but I'm not certain about them. The patients ought to be given every option, yet the cost is horrendous.'

'That's why I wanted you to start this prevention thing. Once people join, they can be sent for automatically for BP and ECG. I wish you'd let me bring my notes.'

'Miranda Mason, I know you're faithful and painstaking, and a damn good nurse, but—'

'That's not what Mary Ann said.'

He looked annoyed. 'That woman passed her medical exams, but there's precious little of the science of life that she could pass in. Whatever she said, it's probably a figment of her imagination.' He took a breath and went on, 'What I want to say is that I've had a long trip. I'm jet-lagged and in need of a shower. But I'm much more in need of a cosy chat with the girl who sees dragons in the mountainsides, and magic in the cherry blossom.'

'Really?' Miranda looked puzzled. 'When I came to Genting I was that sort of girl, very innocent and gullible. But I've grown up a lot, come to know myself. . .'

'Please, dearest Miranda, don't dare to change. I fell for that girl on the cable car, who was honest and open-eyed and lovely in her frank enjoyment of nature, and made me feel young again. Be that girl again? Couldn't you see how much I liked talking to you? I had no intention of staying up all night, that night in the hospital, but it was just sheer magic, being with you. Don't turn into someone else yet, Miranda. I want to take that girl for lunch—all right, a very late lunch, then. Is that a deal? Be honest. If you can't fill the bill, you'd better come clean.'

'Well,' Miranda sat back in amazement, 'I don't know. You'll have to tell me.'

'Then we go out to lunch—nowhere special, don't panic about clothes.'

'I wasn't panicking.'

Jon shook his head with a smile, and she just looked back, bewitched by his eyes, and the way they spoke to her. If only he were serious, and not playing with her! 'You saw yourself as a schoolgirl, I expect. I saw you as a young woman who just happens to have a soul. There, have I expressed myself well?'

'You've paid me a lot of compliments. I thought I was beginning to understand myself, but you haven't really described me among all those nice things you said. I'm much plainer than that.'

He stood up. 'Will you give me five minutes to change? It's such a nice day—you see I'm not used to the sun after autumn in London—I'd like to go for a walk. You haven't anything planned today?'

'No.'

'Then let's walk and talk, and then I'll take you back in good time.'

'That would be lovely.' Miranda sat on the edge of the sofa, her heart rippling with excitement. Jon must be missing that woman he had taken to Switzerland, and be anxious for undemanding female company. She didn't mind at all. Every minute with him was a happy one.

There was just the tiny danger which she had foreseen: she might become too fond of him. But that wasn't likely, because after today they would both be back at work. It was just today. And because it was special, she determined to enjoy every minute. But she hoped Jon would not kiss her, as he had in Genting. It was different up there. Here they were colleagues, and it would be wrong to be more than friends. She was sitting on the very edge of her seat, remembering the way he had taken her face in his hands and kissed her very gently but very long, as though he enjoyed the taste. . .

'What's that smile about?'

She looked up at him, colouring slightly. At one time she would have been shy, but today she laughed and said, 'Secrets, just secrets.'

He was wearing close-fitting fawn slacks and a matching shirt. 'You sure you aren't too tired to walk after all that swimming?'

'No. I've got all my strength back. And you haven't let me thank you for looking after me while I was ill.'

He put his arm about her shoulders. 'Come on. Do you want to powder your nose?'

She escaped from his hold. 'Euphemisms! I'll use your bathroom as you've finished.'

They went down to the car which he had left by the pool. 'Where are you taking me?' she asked.

'The Lake Gardens. It's a lovely walk.'

'Sounds nice. I haven't been there yet.'

'I'm hoping you can conjure up some trolls and elves for me, to make it less boring.' They drove out past the guard, who stood to attention as they passed.

'I hope you won't expect too much. I can't do magic to order,' Miranda laughed.

'That's what you think,' murmured Jon, as they turned off left from the highway and went under a flyover, thunderous with midday traffic. It was a busy city, but there were trees everywhere, and the new Islamic buildings that were going up around the city were gleaming in white latticework and gold minarets.

And then they were driving past an elegant wall, on which the words 'Lake Club' in small iron letters were followed by the new Malaysian name in large wrought-iron letters. Miranda had heard of that. 'You're a member? I thought there was a waiting list and the subscriptions are astronomical.'

Jon smiled as they drew up at a kiosk where the inmate checked the disc on the windscreen. 'There is, and they are.' And they drove past, the man in the kiosk saying, 'Nice to see you, Doctor.'

Unashamed luxury surrounded them. But Jon quickly parked the car, and drew Miranda by the hand away from the smart brick exterior, surrounded by orchids and trailing plants, and they wandered among the tall trees, some palm trees towering higher than the buildings, that must have been there for a hundred years. He talked of colonial days, and the pride of the people, because though they belonged to the Commonwealth they had never been conquered by war, but had been voluntarily under British rule. She could tell his great love of the country and its people. And as always, their conversation flowed as naturally as last time. Miranda's heart was at peace, as they walked slowly, stopping occasionally to admire a flower or a tree, as though they had known each other all their lives.

Having seen the parkland, they walked up towards the club buildings. There were tennis courts first, then they came to the magnificent five-pool swimming complex, where children ran about happily, in the warm sun. 'Makes you thirsty?' queried Jon.

Miranda agreed, and they sat by the pool under an umbrella, and drank refreshing Japanese beer which Jon insisted was hardly alcoholic, but very good for a hot day. Several people recognised him, but he did not engage in conversation, apparently making it clear from the way he sat with his head close to Miranda's that they were a two-some only. 'I could hardly have planned a nicer day for my return to Malaysia than if I'd sat down and thought about it for weeks,' he said.

'That's a lovely compliment. I can say the same. It's been such fun.'

'Have a bite to eat before we go back? That breakfast must have gone by now.'

'Yes, thank you. Just a little.' And she looked at her watch. 'The sun is low. Oh, heavens, Jon, did you know it was six o'clock?'

'No more than you did, my darling. Does it matter? We did need a restful day.' He called her darling as one would a child, or a pet cat, but she liked the sound of it nonetheless.

They walked into the marble entrance hall, and Jonathan was greeted again by several regulars. 'You come here much?' asked Miranda.

'I guess I'm not much of a home bird.' And again, in spite of his wealth, she pitied him. In spite of his women, his fame, his status here, he was lonely. He was well into his thirties, and still walked his path alone. She put her hand into his without being asked. He looked pleased, and squeezed it tight as they went up a flight of handsome stairs.

'We'll eat here. It's quite a simple place.' He led her into one of the many restaurants whose names and arrows were up on the walls. It was dim, and there was a pure white orchid in the centre of each table, translucent in the light, greeny veins tracing the shape of the petals. 'Do you like oysters?'

'I don't know.'

'I think you do.' And he ordered oysters, *ikit kurau*, papaya ice-cream and crêpes Suzette. Miranda smiled, and

allowed him to spoil her, knowing it would do no good to
protest. She could see what he meant—ordering this kind
of food for himself was no fun. Seeing the surprise and
delight on her face was more fun, and she didn't have to
pretend the delight. The entire meal was superb.

Miranda had lost count of time again, but by now she
didn't care. 'I think this has been the loveliest day of my
life,' she told him.

'It isn't over yet.' Jon drove her home through the well
lit streets, and once more back to Peninsula Court. For
the first time she began to be apprehensive.

'Why are we here? It's getting late.'

He parked the car and came round to her side, opening
the door and taking her hand to help her out. 'Don't be
afraid, darling. I'm not a louse.'

'I didn't mean—oh yes, I did.' It was so wonderful to
be with someone she could speak frankly to. 'I mean, what
is there to come back to? I thought you'd take me home.'

'There are two things to come back to—and then I'll
keep my promise and take you home early. See, it's only
nine. We won't be long.'

On the way up in the lift, Miranda said, 'Are you going
to tell me what two things?'

'Well, coffee, for one.'

'I see.' She said no more, as the guard was listening. They
shook off their shoes and went into the lounge. 'Oh, Jonathan!' she exclaimed.

'That's the other. I knew you'd like it.' It was the view
of the city by night. Jon had switched on a coffee-maker,
and came over to put his arm loosely round her shoulders.
'Like it?'

'It's unspeakably beautiful!'

'See any trolls or goblins?'

'No. But I'm pretty sure there must be fairies in that
golden palace.'

'That's the King's palace—more armed guards than
fairies, I guess.' He drew her to sit down. 'Now, will you

have Irish coffee, Caribbean coffee or Jamaican coffee?'

'Whatever you recommend. You seem to know how to please me.'

'I do? I'm glad.' He poured the coffee into beautiful glasses, added liqueur, and a dash of cream. 'Try that, Princess.'

She turned sharply. 'Now why did you call me that?'

'Don't know,' he admitted. 'You aren't an ordinary girl, I suppose. Does it matter?'

'No. Only it was Jake's name for me.' And her voice was low as she remembered how fond she was of dear Jake.

'Sorry.' Jon turned away and walked to the other side of the room with his coffee, setting it down on a sideboard.

Miranda was suddenly distressed to have said such an idiotic thing. She put her glass down and ran over to him. 'You see what a stupid creature I am? Jon, I didn't mean to be so crass—'

He pulled her into his arms in a fierce and longing hug. She clung to his firm back, her cheek against his chest, returning his embrace wholeheartedly. And then his lips found hers as she looked up eagerly, closed her eyes and accepted his warm mobile kiss, a kiss such as he had never given her in Genting. This was what she had been afraid of. But now she was not afraid at all, but joyful and exhilarated to be in his arms, generous and passionate in response. He murmured to her between kisses, but there wasn't enough time for her to know what he was saying. But they were tender sweet things that she welcomed, like the words he had whispered to her when she was delirious. But now she was well, and she knew he was saying those things as though he meant them.

She neither wanted nor expected that he would stop kissing her so very abruptly, but he moved away from her as sharply as they had come together, and left her with her head spinning so much that she stumbled and grabbed hold of a chair to hold her. Jon had turned with his back to her. She moved round the chair, still holding it, and sat down, looking sightlessly out across the sea of lights that was the city beneath them. He stayed where he was for some moments. Miranda caught her breath, trying not to let him hear her.

In a low voice she said, 'I'd better go now.'

He turned. 'I'll take you.'

'I can walk.'

'Don't be silly. That place is full of muggers.'

'I did tell you I was silly.' She had never felt so miserable. 'I'm sorry. It—it was all my fault.'

He was silent again, and she ventured to look across. Their faces were lit only by the city outside, apart from concealed lighting at each side of the picture window. In a gruffish voice Jon said, 'I'm sorry too.'

'I told you we should have talked about my health club.'

He seemed more sure of himself then, moving back to the window and looking down at her. 'You were right. I want to thank you for the day. It was nice, and I appreciate you giving up your time at my whim.'

'I enjoyed it too.' In a small voice she added, 'All of it.' And as he sat down next to her, she said, 'Especially the papaya ice-cream.'

'You said that on purpose to try to sound childish!'

'Ah, but you'll never know if it was on purpose or not.'

'You witch. You little witch!'

And she knew they were in danger of again making the mistake of getting too close. It would be foolish. Jon had his woman, his affair of the heart, and she had no right to interfere with that. She had no wish to. He would only blame her if she messed up his life any more. She had seen how lonely he was, how he would like to settle down. Maybe this woman in England was the one. She mustn't selfishly allow her own desires to spoil his hopes for a happy future.

So against her real wishes, she said, 'Time I went, please, Jon.'

'Right. Finished your coffee?'

Miranda drained the rich liquid, savouring the last drop. 'That was the most delicious meal I've ever had in my life.' She picked up her bag. 'Ready.'

'We'll do it again some time.'

She made no answer to that. It would be nice if he did ask her again, but somehow she thought not. They got on so well—and yet there was something that held her back. They went down in the lift without speaking. As they got into the car, Jon said, 'We seem to have talked all day.'

'As opposed to all night when we were in Genting Hospital.'

'The last time I did that was at university. We used to sit up drinking coffee and discussing philosophy and the meaning of life.' He smiled down at her, back to his usual cheerful self. 'Now that's a subject we didn't get on to today. Next time, remind me to ask you the meaning of life.'

'After we've discussed the new health club.'

He drew up outside the nurses' home. 'I won't drive in, there won't be any muggers in the garden, but go right in so that I can see you're all right.'

'Goodnight, Jon,' Miranda said softly.

'Goodnight.' She heard the soft smooth tones of his voice still in her ears as she went indoors without looking back. She threw her bag on the bed, and ran to the window for one last glimpse of the green Rover by the light of the yellow street lamp. There goes a good man, she thought. There goes my obsession. . . And she tried to think back over what they had said. Conversation had flowed so easily, as though their minds worked in the same way. Jon had talked about himself a lot—yet was she any the wiser? She didn't know why he wasn't married. She didn't even know which university he had been at, or at which hospital was the symposium he had just been to.

Miranda shook her head. It was obvious that he was just too clever to give too much away. And she, blithely innocent, had told him about everything, even to the stream in the garden at home, and the apple tree in the corner of the garden. Next time—if there was a next time—she would watch herself, wait until he revealed himself more before she did the same. If there was a next time. . .

It was very hot, and she turned the fan up to full. In his apartment, and in the Lake Club, the air-conditioning was just perfect. One could forget the tropical heat, and just relax. Would she ever be rich enough to afford that sort of living?

That proved to be just the antidote to her dreaming about Jonathan's kisses. She would work hard to be a success in her own right. She had already saved a substantial amount from her work at Genting. The salary at the Devereux was excellent, and if she ran the new health club as well, she would have a decent sum to invest. Miranda went to sleep contented, with no regretful longing for Jon Smith, but visions of M Mason, tycoon. . .

CHAPTER ELEVEN

FROM that day onwards, Miranda began to enjoy Kuala Lumpur. She had a good and profitable job to do, that took all her organisational skill as well as her nursing experience. And she was reading the financial weeklies too, enlarging her knowledge of stocks and shares, ready for when she had a sizeable enough sum to invest.

Her relationship with Jonathan was warm but businesslike. There were no more candlelight dinners for two, although he often stopped by and talked for hours, about the Klinik, about the Good Health Club, and about things in general.

They had redecorated the physio department, and made it into a real gymnasium, with all the equipment not only for physiotherapy, but for keeping fit. They had several exercise bicycles, sets of weights, isometric bars and chest expanders. Miranda had asked for and got a small computer. She had a small office where she kept the records for the club, and she worked there three days a week, spending the rest of the time in normal nursing duties.

It was only by accident that she overheard Leonie Lister complaining about the club. Miranda had just come in from the pool, where she had been for half an hour after work. Leonie was in someone's room at the nurses' home, and the door was open.

'It really is too bad! That club is lowering the whole tone of the Klinik. It used to be a reputable hospital, but now it's full of middle-aged people thinking only of their figures. I even overheard one woman making a date with someone who wasn't her husband. It's disgusting! And

Jonathan can't see it, now that he's besotted with that woman.'

Miranda was going to creep past, when the other girl said, 'Come on, Leonie. It's a good thing, even if we've only stopped one person from furring up their arteries. Prevention should be encouraged. The patients' morals are their own affair.'

'Mark my words, this place will get a reputation if it goes on like this!'

The other girl, Jackie, said, 'Easy—ask Miranda to segregate the sexes. Have men and women on different days.'

'I suppose I'll have to.' Leonie's voice sounded menacing, cold. Miranda walked past, her bare feet dry now in the heat.

So when Leonie stalked into the club next morning, Miranda had a good idea what the conversation was to be about, and was ready for the criticism. 'Hello, Leonie,' she smiled.

'Morning. How's life in the massage parlour?'

Miranda looked up from the computer, smiling sweetly. 'Which massage parlour is that, Leonie?'

Leonie sniffed. 'You just don't realise that this place is only one step away from a brothel.'

'Good lord, is it really?' Miranda refused to be riled.

'You know it is. I was never in favour of going ahead with this. Do you know I heard a couple making an assignation last time I was here? I think it's a terrible thing for the Devereux Klinik to have degenerated into a place like this. It used to be one of the best places in town, but now you might as well call it the whorehouse.'

Miranda coloured. That was a bit strong! And she was no longer the timid and wide-eyed innocent. 'That's a lie,' she snapped. 'And if you don't like it, please complain to your superiors, who happen to think prevention is an excellent idea. The doctors are delighted with the way this has turned out. We've identified eight people so far with dangerously high BPs, and they've been treated in time.

Eight people who might easily have been stroke patients.'

'I'm not saying that's a bad thing—'

'You don't know enough about what we do. Look, the computer stores the names, and recalls them every six months. They only come for physio if they want to. Most of them think it's a good thing, and come. It's a sort of medical insurance.' Miranda pressed a key of the computer and a list of names and ages came up. 'There are your sinners, Leonie. Most of them over fifty. All are overweight, and all they care about is getting down to a healthy weight. Well?'

'But I definitely heard that woman—'

'You heard one person. Might it not be a patient making an appointment with her dentist? I've got three dentists and six doctors on my books. Making a date with someone isn't necessarily wicked.'

A patient came in then, and Leonie Lister went away without another word. Miranda was troubled. It was miserable when someone made rubbish of something she valued and was proud of. She heard Rasa with someone in the gym, and walked over to watch. Rasa turned round and said, 'Oh, look, Miranda. Mr Kuan is so much better. I've just told him he's my star patient.' Mr Kuan had been referred to the club following a stroke. He was tiny, with yellowing parchment skin and bright black buttons of eyes, that twinkled with fun and relief that his disability had been overcome. Jonathan had replaced the artery in the neck with a small piece from the blood vessel in the thigh, and Mr Kuan, sixty years old, was as active as a youngster. He was pedalling away on the smallest exercise bike. Rasa cautioned, 'Steady! Don't overdo it.'

He stopped, and beamed. He was wearing a vest and shorts, and his grizzled parchment face was damp with sweat. 'Sister, I feel so good. Better than I have for years.'

'Then I shall discharge you,' joked Miranda.

His face fell. 'Then I'll have nothing to look forward to.'

She laughed. 'Only joking. Would you like to come twice a month?'

'Can't I come weekly?'

'Of course. There are no rules how often. It's up to you.' And as she entered his name on the weekly list, Miranda wished Leonie had been there. If anyone could give the place respectability it was Mr Kuan; he was an Episcopalian minister.

Later she said to Rasa, 'I think Leonie must come and meet Mr Kuan.' She explained what the Sister had said about their club.

'There's no secret about why she's against you,' said Rasa. 'Jon Smith has stopped taking her out since you arrived. She's just plain jealous.'

'But—' Miranda felt herself blushing, 'I'm not going out with him either. We went to the Lake Club once, but I've hardly spoken to him since except about business matters.'

'It isn't your fault. She's been trying to get him for years—tried every trick. But he's honourable. As soon as he found out she had a husband, even though they're separated, he stopped seeing her. And she blames you.'

'That's silly,' protested Miranda.

'Maybe. But you know he's taken a week off to go to Genting soon?'

'Yes.' Jon had said he was going. And she herself was planning to spend her final week up there, holidaying with Bill, Jake and Maidie. She didn't mention that. She didn't want the year to end so quickly.

'Leonie was certain he would take her,' Rasa went on. 'So everyone is waiting to see. It's a tense situation.'

'It sure is,' Miranda agreed.

'We have usually known by now who it would be. They would have been seen eating out together, or she would call and wait for him. This time it's different. There's no one hanging about, and he always eats alone.'

Miranda couldn't help giggling. 'Poor man! Does he know you have a tail on him?'

Rasa joined in the laughter. 'But it isn't like that. Only there are just a limited number of restaurants and clubs here, so people are bound to be seen.'

'Mary Ann Moon still works there.' Miranda was thinking out loud. 'But Jon doesn't think very much of her now.' And she felt a stab of genuine jealousy as she remembered the way those two had been close, the first time she met them.

Rasa said, 'Leonie thought she had it made till you turned up.'

'Well, he isn't asking me. And if you think it would make Leonie happy, you have my permission to tell her that.'

'Okay, I might. But it's fun to keep her guessing. Most of the girls would like to see the great Leonie taken down a peg or two.'

Miranda shook her finger. 'Behave yourself, Rasa, or I'll tell her myself.'

They were both laughing when a man's voice asked, 'Tell who what?'

Rasa melted away into the background immediately as Jonathan came in, pulling off his mask and cap after a session operating. He sat on the corner of the desk, and Miranda looked down, hoping he would ask no more questions about their conversation. She pretended to be checking something on the screen. Softly he said, 'Miranda?' and his voice turned her heart right over her breast. She looked up then, unable to pretend any more that she was uninterested in his presence. He knew her too well. If she tried to pretend, he would see through her. He smiled into her eyes, and she knew the aching truth, that she could spend the rest of her life close to that familiar, wonderful face and never tire of him. However many women he had, however many conquests he made, he had the power over her that was more shattering than anything she had ever known in her life. Even now, with the stories of Leonie still ringing in her ears. . .

'If you can spare a moment, I'd like to have a chat with you about this club of yours, how it's going,' said Jon. 'I know it's swanning along at present, by all accounts, but my dear, you won't be here for ever, unfortunately, and it's probably time we trained someone else to take over. I understand there've been a few unfortunate rumours—'

Miranda's love did not prevent her from sitting up straight, looking him in the eye, and saying very firmly, 'And I know where you've been getting these fairy stories from too.'

'You do?' His voice was soft and teasing again, and she was glad she was sitting down, as her knees would have turned to water. 'Well, look, Sister—it's obviously a long story, and needs some sorting out. We'll go over the whole thing at my place. You've no objection? Be ready in half an hour, would you—and bring all the balance sheets?' And without giving her any time to accept or refuse he had gone.

Miranda sat at her desk as though hypnotised. It was just as well she was leaving soon; her feelings were getting a trifle too strong for comfort. She opened her bag, fingering the return air ticket to Heathrow. She would soon be carried away from this intense situation where she could no longer control her own feelings—back to dear dirty old London. And on to leafy little Alston Magna. This episode in her life would soon be forgotten, once she was back in harness. Just then Rasa came in. 'Shall I lock up?' she asked. She said nothing about Jonathan, for which Miranda was grateful.

'I'll do it,' Miranda told her.

'Don't forget the balance sheets.'

'Rasa Khalid, you were listening!'

'The door was open,' Rasa explained.

Miranda smiled up at her friend. 'Well, if anyone asks you—and from what I see, everyone will—this is a business meeting, called because I'm leaving soon. And if Leonie Lister wants to know, Mr Devereux-Smith is my employer and nothing but my employer, and I intend to keep it that way.'

'Has he ever kissed you?' Rasa leaned on the desk, her thin face innocent. 'I won't tell.'

'Yes. Just as a friend.' Miranda knew the colour was coming to her cheeks and envied her friend for her olive-dark skin.

'But you were there ages last time.'

'How do you know?'

'Jackie's sister is engaged to Wong, the gateman at Peninsula Court.' So it really was almost impossible to keep any secrets here. Miranda smiled. At least she had been warned now. Wong would report back how long she stayed with Jonathan tonight. She must keep track of the time. Easier said than done when Jon turned on his magic. . .

She knew she had mellowed a lot since her first days in Malaysia. She knew she was a woman now, self-controlled and certain what she wanted in life. She was no longer afraid of speaking her mind. Yet she also knew that Jonathan Smith was the one man—the only person—in the whole world who could manipulate her, because of the effect he had on her inner private emotions. And she had to admit to herself that her emotions were far less controllable than her mind. Jon knew—who better than he, who had such a list of conquests to his name that everyone knew of them—how to look at her, touch her, modulate his voice—in a way to get through that newly acquired veneer of sophistication and calm.

Rasa said goodnight. Miranda said after her retreating back, 'A business meeting.' Why was Rasa in such a hurry? She had appeared to want to chat at first.

Then she found out. 'Ready, darling?' Jon's deep voice. Rasa must have seen him coming. There had been no need at all to call her darling, even if he did with most women.

'Just about. The balance sheets, you said?' She put them tidily in her briefcase. 'Ready.' She turned her face up to him, determined to keep calm and efficient and controlled. Jon bent and kissed her. It was a very light, gentle butterfly touch of a kiss, as though she were very dear to him. 'That wasn't necessary,' she said, standing up and picking up her shoulder bag with the briefcase.

'Sorry. Couldn't help it,' he replied, looking very unsorry.

'What a Don Juan you are!' Maybe mockery was the best way to deal with him.

He smiled at that. 'Not all the time.'

'I thought you kept that sort of thing for Genting.'

They walked slowly round the corner of the building, past the swimming pool. Jon took her elbow in a casual, friendly way as they walked to the car. 'Yes, I do. Business and pleasure as far apart as possible.'

That was encouraging. Tonight they were to talk business. Good. As they got in the car, Miranda said, 'You really ought to settle down.'

Jon stared the engine. 'I'm smart—I steer clear of all the grasping gold-diggers I meet. The trouble is, I steer clear of everyone else as well.'

'Why?'

'It started at university. If you want to hear my sob story, I was a mere kid—wet behind the ears where girls were concerned. Someone with a lot more knowledge than I got her claws in me. I went through hell for that woman—believed everything she said about killing herself if I left her, you know the sort of thing. How I coped with my work I don't know.' He was silent for a moment as he filtered into the traffic flow. 'Maybe work saved me. I put my heart and soul into it, went to work in an outlying hospital where she didn't see me every day—and bingo, she met someone else while I was away.'

'Now I understand,' said Miranda softly.

'Do you? Maybe you do, love. You have an understanding sort of nature. So you see, I found out the hard way what having claws meant. I didn't mean to let it happen again.'

'I'm really sorry I said you were a Don Juan. You aren't at all.'

'I'm not?'

'No. You don't set out to hurt people.'

'That's true. I don't go out with vulnerable types. You may have noticed.'

She was silent as they approached his apartment block. She was vulnerable, but fair enough, he hadn't made any pass at her. Not really. By now she was completely on his side. Yet even then a tiny voice was warning her that he knew how to touch a woman's heart. In the apartment she must touch no alcohol, and sit at the opposite side of the room while they worked.

As they arrived, Miranda smiled at the gateman. 'His name is Wong and he's courting Jackie's sister,' she explained.

'My gateman? No wonder that Lister woman seemed to know my every move!'

'Leonie? I thought you were friends.'

'You remember what I was saying about claws?' Jon didn't need to say more. On the watch for claws all his life. Poor Jon! For a second Miranda remembered how he had looked into her eyes, that day on the cable car. How their gaze had intertwined as though their very souls were being laid bare in that one brief encounter. Did he see someone who didn't have the ability to grow claws?

'Here we are,' he said.

'You don't have to remind me. I'll remember this place and its fabulous view when I'm stuck in the rush hour in a London tube.'

He didn't play games with her. Inside the apartment he went straight across to the sideboard and poured two small gin slings. 'Make yourself comfortable. I'd like a shower. If you feel the same, there's a bathroom off the spare bedroom. We'll work better if we're fresh.'

It was a sticky night. Miranda went into his second bathroom and let the shower run very cold over her body, revitalising her after the long day. There was a fluffy white bathrobe in there, but she had come to a business meeting, and a white bathrobe might not be terribly sensible. She gave her dress a good shake, and put it on again, then brushed her hair. It was getting long. She had been so busy with her work that she hadn't bothered to get it cut. She had deliberately not bothered with make-up. She was not here to look attractive, but to talk about profit and loss.

She was standing looking at the view when Jonathan came back, wearing jeans and a tee-shirt, his hair still damp. His blue eyes were serious as he helped himself to his unfinished drink, apparently intent on getting down to work. Reassured, Miranda spread her papers on the coffee table and Jonathan sat beside her. 'Now, what have you got for me?' he asked.

She realised that they were close together and drinking gin—both her good resolutions gone already! But he was playing fair, waiting for her to explain what she had brought.

'I can't give you any final figures,' she told him. 'We're charging by the month at present, but we were thinking of making a yearly subscription. It would make the accounting easier.'

Jon pulled a paper towards him. 'Is that all you're charging?'

'It's a fair average. We checked with similar places.'

'My clinic isn't average, it's the best. That should be reflected in the prices.'

'But—' she began.

'In Malaysia, Miranda, that's how it's done. People value you at your price. They don't think they've had good treatment unless they've paid a lot for it.'

'Fair enough. What do you suggest, then?' She made a note to revise the fees.

'Start at the beginning of the next financial year—oh, you won't be with us then. Make a note to charge the earth annually. We can have a refund system for those who don't use all the facilities.' Jon didn't seem at all perturbed that she wouldn't be here, and Miranda felt a stab of regret as she wrote.

He was a businessman all right. 'Anything else?' she asked.

'Yes. Do you like *nasi limak*?'

'I do very much. My favourite Malaysian dish.'

'Good. I ordered some to be sent up when you went to shower.'

'I see.' She hoped he would get back to work soon. She felt an irresistible urge to nestle against his shoulder when his warmth and masculinity was so very close. He showed no sign of moving, however, and she daren't, so their bodies kept touching as they worked.

He put the list of fees down. 'Now then, we have to choose someone to take over from you, so that the whole thing goes on running smoothly when you leave. Have you anyone in mind?' He leaned back casually, letting his arm rest on the back of the sofa behind her head. She only had to sit back a trifle, and she would touch him. . .

'Rasa knows all about it,' she told him.

'But we need her in the gym. I want a desk wallah.'

'Not senior to Rasa?'

'Certainly not. Someone she can work with as well as she does with you.'

'One of the nurses?' asked Miranda.

'I was thinking of Leonie Lister—if you approve.'

'Good lord! She's our greatest critic, Jonathan!' she protested.

'Right. In my experience, give someone a job to do, and within a week they're as proud as Punch. You think that might work with Leonie?'

'Yes, I do. She doesn't like me much, though.'

Jonathan smiled. His hand came down and ruffled her hair for a second. 'She isn't too keen on me either. She's a hysterical female of the very worst type claw-wise—but she's capable and clever, and I believe could do this job well. She'll be in the one place where to criticise the club would be to criticise herself. And it gets her out of my hair,' he added quietly.

Miranda turned to him spontaneously. 'That's so devious!'

'I know. But will it work?'

'I'll do my best for you.'

'Thanks, kid.' The doorbell rang then, and Jon went to bring back two platefuls of *nasi limak*, steaming and smelling like paradise. 'Dinner is served,' said Jon.

Miranda ran to fetch napkins and forks. 'You want chilli sauce, Jon? You know it's pretty hot already?'

'I know. Allow me this my one vice.'

'Your *one*?' Miranda smiled, but she meant it.

Jonathan sat up straight by her. 'Now what do you mean by that barbed comment?' He watched her sit with her meal. 'Oh, I know. Of course—I'm the great sinner, aren't I?' He went across the room and switched on a tape, and the overture to Mozart's *Don Giovanni* came tumbling out into the spacious apartment. The stylised Viennese notes seemed slightly strange in this Oriental setting. Jonathan said, his eyes on Miranda, 'The man who goes to hell and horrible torment for monkeying around with women.'

Miranda had been looking forward to her meal; now she laid down her fork. 'Jonathan, I didn't mean that was you—truly.'

'Then what other vices do you charge me with?'

The music filled the room. Miranda felt uncomfortable. 'Please turn it off,' she asked quietly.

He obeyed. In the sudden silence they could hear the cicadas in the garden below. 'Tell me, what do you charge me with?' he asked.

She excused herself, her voice very quiet. 'You're—not heartless. Giovanni's sin was that he despised women, used them, and I don't think you do that.'

'Thank you, Miranda,' he said quietly. 'Thank you for that.'

She looked at him then, and saw such tenderness in his beloved face that she looked away quickly, and tried to think of the magic view that stretched out before them.

He said, 'Eat, woman. There's nothing so awful as a congealed fried egg on cold coconut rice.' They ate, and the atmosphere calmed between them. Jon said as he ate, 'You've finished all attempts to discredit me, then?'

'No discredit. You're a good man, Jon. I believe that.'

His voice softened again. 'I just like wine, women and gambling?'

Miranda laughed. 'Don't bully me, Jon! Don't put words into my mouth.'

'What kind of man would be good enough for this princess, then? What has Zendik got that other mortals haven't?'

Miranda felt poleaxed. She knew Jon must have heard the rumours of her night with Zendik, but he had never mentioned it before. She had thought it forgotten. Face flaming, she stood up. 'I must go,' she said hastily.

'I didn't want to send you away.'

'You succeeded.' She stood at the door, waiting for him to open it. He came to her, eyes concerned, but she turned her face away, murmuring, 'You know how easy it is to con a kid like me.'

He didn't reply at once. Then in a very low voice he said, 'Is that what he did?'

Miranda faced him, wanting him to know the truth. 'I was so gullible I was ridiculous. He said he missed his wife and children—needed someone understanding to be with!' She spat out the words. 'Now take me home.'

'Did he rape you?'

'Yes, I think so.' Hot tears coursed down her cheeks. 'He thought all Western girls were like that.' And, in some sort of anguished justice, 'He apologised.'

Jonathan reached out and took her in his arms. She made no protest. She was glad he knew the truth. She thought she heard him say, 'Oh, my poor darling,' but she wasn't sure, because her heart's blood was beating in her ears.

In the distance the phone rang politely. Neither of them moved at first, but Jonathan went to answer it. Miranda took the opportunity of dashing away her tears with her handkerchief, and composing herself. She heard him say, 'Yes, she's here.' He turned, his eyes compassionate. 'For you, love—your friend at Genting.'

'Bill?' She took the receiver. 'Hello? Bill? How did you find me?'

'They all seemed to know where you were.' His voice gave nothing away. 'Sorry to disturb you.'

'Nothing to apologise for. We've just had a meeting—business meeting—and I'm on the way home.'

'Okay. We're all coming over for the day tomorrow. Is that okay?'

'Wonderful!' she exclaimed.

'All right to pick you up about eleven?'

Miranda's emotional trauma faded, at the prospect of meeting her friends. 'I have to go, Jon,' she said, when Bill had rung off.

'I'll take you.'

'Get a cab for me—you know how they talk.'

'I'll drop you a block away.'

He dropped her a block away. They had said nothing on the way. Miranda thanked him, and he reached across to open the door for her. 'I'm glad we sorted things out.' He drove away rather fast.

CHAPTER TWELVE

MIRANDA was appalled at the way she had given away
secrets about herself to Jonathan. True, he had been
sympathetic and kind, but it was a private matter
between herself and Zendik. After all, Jon gave away no
secrets about himself and his lady friend in England, his
'affair of the heart'. She was uncomfortable with
wounded pride, mortified at the ease with which she
opened her heart to him.

And so it was that she threw herself into a hectic day
of enjoyment with her friends. The three of them had
hired a car, and driven down to KL. 'I've just gotta have
some new gowns,' Maidie insisted. 'The engagement
party is going to be the biggest thing since sliced bread.'

'Mary Ann Moon and Mr Heng?'

'Sure. You better make sure you come up by then.'

Miranda made some calculations. 'Yes, I can arrange
that. I'm glad I won't miss it, it should be fun.'

'Something special.' Jake didn't sound enthusiastic,
but then wild enthusiasm wasn't his style. 'There's a
coupla groups coming up for the night. Oh, and Zen's
coming up, with his band.' He tossed off the remark, but
Miranda was grateful to know. She would be prepared,
should she meet Zendik accidentally.

Bill was driving. He jumped out to give Miranda a kiss
on the cheek. 'Look, I've got to deliver my gear to Kim's
place. Want to come, or shall I meet you?'

Maidie explained, 'Bill's already left us. He's spending his last few days with Kim.'

'Yes, I've done my stint at the Empress,' said Bill, 'and
very nice it was too. But I'm on holiday for the rest of

the year. I'll meet you at the airport. Leave your luggage too, Kim's man will see to it for us.'

Everything seemed to be moving very fast, all of a sudden. 'I want to go home, but—it's been good here. I hope we come back,' Miranda said.

'Yeah.' Bill was so much more assured than when they had come up—neatly dressed, the perfect businessman. 'I came up for the money—and boy, I've got more that I expected of that! It's going to make a difference back home. I can wait a while, pick up a good job instead of taking the first that comes along.'

Miranda laughed at him. 'Bill, you know you've picked up Maidie's accent?'

Bill looked down at Maidie and gave her a quick squeeze. 'Boy, I'm gonna miss this little broad!' Their mutual smiles showed only friendship. Miranda stole a look at Jake. His face was calm, but he caught her anxious stare, and gave her a big wink to show that everything was all right.

They had a long cheerful lunch at Kim's hotel in the tourist area of the city. They talked over old times, and planned what the next years would bring, and if they would meet again.

'Why don't you and Maidie come and see me in Alston Magna?' Miranda suggested.

Jake grinned. 'Why not? Send us an invitation to your wedding.'

'Wedding? Me? Didn't I tell you about my plans to be something big in the City?' Miranda dismissed his suggestion with a wave of her hand. And there was more than a grain of truth in what she said. She had planned to invest her money, and try to start a health club similar to the one at the Devereux. She knew she must throw herself into some new venture as soon as she got back, to prevent her dwelling on the happy times she had had in Jonathan's hospital.

Afterwards, the girls spent some time in the dress shops. Maidie bought two shimmering gowns, suitable

for performances, and Miranda decided to treat herself
to a pretty evening dress for the engagement party. They
laughed and giggled quite a lot, and paraded in several
model dresses while making up their minds. It was a
happy day. Miranda went back to the nurses' home with
her shiny carrier bag, the luxury chiffon wrapped in rus-
tling tissue paper.

She met Jackie in the home, and they went out together
to eat, as they often did. Jackie revealed the fact that
Leonie had been informed of her 'promotion' in taking
over the health club—and was already becoming enthusiastic about promoting good diet and good living. 'She's
even stopped talking about going to Genting with Jonathan. It's pretty obvious now that there isn't anyone
going with him this time,' said Jackie.

'And she doesn't mind?'

'She looks ahead,' smiled Jackie. 'If not this time, then
maybe the next.'

Miranda looked down. 'Poor Jonathan!'

'What's poor about Devereux-Smith?'

'Like the Flying Dutchman—doomed to go on from
year to year with nothing to stop him—nothing to hold
him. . . Unless maybe that woman he took to Switzerland. . .'

The next week was busy, because Miranda was showing Leonie the ropes as well as preparing for her own last
days in Genting. She was going before Jonathan, and in
a way, she hoped their paths would not cross. It would
be embarrassing—and it would remind her how much
she still cared for him.

And then on the Friday evening, she took her luggage
to Kim's place and went back to say goodbye to the
Devereux Klinik. She promised to keep in touch with
Rasa, said goodbye to the other girl, then tapped politely on Jonathan's door. 'Come in,' he answered.

She went in. She had not been looking forward to saying goodbye to him. 'You are off now?' asked Jonathan.

'Yes. I promised to have dinner with my friends at the Empress.'

'Better hurry, then.' He looked at his watch. He was in his shirt-sleeves with a pile of notes in front of him, and a microphone, dictating letters. Then a hint of a smile, a touch of humour appeared in his eyes. 'You're taking the *kabel cerata*? Watch those mountain caves, then.'

Miranda managed to smile back. 'Goodbye, Jonathan. Good luck.'

He stood up, came round the desk, and shook her hand very briefly. 'Goodbye, love. I can never thank you enough for all the good work you've put in here. We'll miss you.'

She had perhaps hoped for a more effusive farewell, but there was none. He turned to go back to his work, and Miranda made a quick exit, her eyes misty because of all the things she wanted to say and couldn't find the words. Suddenly glad he had kept it simple, she ran out with her one canvas bag of luggage, to the waiting cab.

As it wound its way round the lower slopes of the mountain, she allowed herself to think how much she would miss everyone at the Devereux, but especially Jon. She knew it would be hard to forget him. They had talked so much about so many things they had in common. . . How could he slip from her thoughts when he was a part of them so often?'

The car park at the cable station was almost deserted. There was no monsoon tonight. The air was calm and warm, the sky studded with diamonds. Miranda slung her bag on her shoulder, paid the cabby, and walked up to pay her dollar at the office and wait for the tiny car to descend from the clouds—except tonight there were no clouds, and it was possible to see the lighted speck right up there on the side of the precipice. It made her feel unimportant, because the cliffs were so immense, so silent, so magnificent.

There were only a few people on the car. The hooter sounded, eerie in the darkness, echoing from side to side of the valley. Miranda sat down on the wooden seat, staring down at the floor. Even the knowledge of how far down it was had no effect on her. She was thinking of how deep was her love, and how difficult it would be to get it out of her system. And then the conductress said something in Malay, unlocked the door to let a late-comer in. Miranda did not look up at first, then she realised that the newcomer had left a green Rover in the car park. Then she knew. And as she raised her eyes, they met the cool blue stare of her ex-employer. There was no mistaking those broad shoulders, even in the dimness at the other side of the *cerata*.

On his way to Genting to relax. Yet for once he was alone. She heard the conductress laugh, then say, 'This one definitely the prettiest, Doctor,' and she realised that they meant her. Was she to be Jonathan's latest con-quest? She shifted uncomfortably, shivered, and took out an angora sweater as the altitude made it cooler. Jon was at her side at once, helping her to put it on. 'Miranda, please don't look at me as though I'm suffering from some unspeakable skin disease!'

'Sorry,' she muttered.

'Is it because you think I did this deliberately?'

'Didn't you?'

'Well—yes.'

She found herself smiling a little wanly. 'I might have known!' She faced him honestly. 'I can't pretend with you. You know I'm glad to see you.'

'Thank you for that. I promise not to get in your way on your last holiday.' He was silent for a moment, as the car jolted its way over another pylon. Then he said, 'It will seem awfully empty without you.'

'But you'll be going back to England soon, I know.'

He smiled. 'You mean the nurses' Mafia has been spying on me again?'

'No, not exactly. But the story is that you stayed longer in England because of—someone special. It follows that if she's special you'll be going back soon.'

Jon looked at her, his eyes crinkling at the corners. 'All these rumours! I'm going to have to do something drastic about the speculation about me.'

'I suppose they think anyone is fair game.'

'Anyone eligible?'

She nodded. Any conversation with Jon turned into a gentle bantering. It was nice. How she would miss him. . .

The *cerata* trembled slightly as it slowed down before docking. Jon said, 'Your Jake is there. Have a good trip.'

He disappeared within minutes of landing. Miranda turned to see where he had gone. Jake said, 'Hi, pardner. Looking for someone? He just made off for the Casino.'

'Oh.' They walked along the corridor, his hand on her shoulder.

'Glad to be back?' he asked.

She smiled up at her elongated companion. 'Oh yes. About time I heard some decent singing!'

He squeezed her shoulder. 'Okay, Princess. Any requests?'

'Sing "The Black Hills of Dakota." It will remind me of the black mountain of Genting, with the Flame of the Forest trees.'

'Lost my heart in the Black Hills. . .' Jake looked at her with a query.

'Rubbish! How's Suzy? Still in love with Hassan?' She changed the subject as they went into the Empress and straight over to the bar. Suzy was welcoming, and Miranda began to feel at home again. But all the time she was wondering where Jon was, and if she was going to bump into him with some glamorous female he had met in the Casino.

Suzy was anxious to explain what complicated preparations were being made for the engagement party. 'See

how they start the decorations already?' Workmen were
stringing up glittering tinsel garlands. The already ornate
foyer was looking even more lavish and luxurious. 'It will
be the night of the year.' She leaned over to say, 'One
bottle of champagne on every table—free. And Zendik
is flying over from Jakarta to sing specially for them.'

Mr Heng had not seemed to be the romantic type, yet
the gossip was that he had bought Mary Ann a diamond
the size of Elizabeth Taylor's. 'So they are very happy?'
asked Miranda.

Suzy nodded. 'I never saw Dr Moon so happy.'

Jake said, 'She's found what she wants in life—sheer
unadulterated luxury. I'm told they're going round the
world for their honeymoon.'

'Who'll look after the Empress?'

'Heng's son, Kim, and Sister da Costa.'

Cherry Tan came running up. 'Miranda! Do you know
I am going to be chief bridesmaid?'

'Wonderful! And Kim is best man. I think I could do
some matchmaking there!' Miranda laughed.

Cherry said, 'I hear Jonathan Smith is back.'

'Is he?'

'Miranda, you knew very well! Is he a good boss?'

Miranda launched into a detailed account of the Good
Health Club that soon had Cherry changing the subject.
And then Jake got bored as the girls started to talk about
what dresses they were to wear to the party.

Miranda went along with Maidie and Jake—back now
in the Orchid Room. It was good to be back. Then she
saw Jonathan sitting alone at a small table at the back
of the room, and it was hard to be cheerful after that.
Jake eventually saw where she was looking. Without
saying anything to her, he went across the room and
brought Jon back with him. 'Look who's here, girls!
Can't let him dine alone now, can we?' They ordered
Miranda's favourite crab and papaya salad. The talk was
easy, but Jonathan said little. Miranda couldn't relax,

and wished he had chosen some other restaurant to eat in.

While Jake and Maidie were up front, Jon moved round to sit next to Miranda. She had forgotten she had made a request, and when Jake's lovely expressive voice sang, 'Take me back to the Black Hills,' she spent the entire song staring down at her empty plate. Jonathan waited until the singers came back to the table before standing politely and saying goodnight.

It could never be the same again. Miranda knew, as Jonathan left the gorgeous room, that those early carefree days could not be repeated. Experience had intervened. The thrill of her first meeting with Jake had cooled. She could never forget what it had been, but today it was routine. All the same, meeting Jake had been special. Zendik, no. Jake—definitely yes.

Jonathan stayed out of her hair. She didn't see him again, except for once, when she spotted him on the tennis court, taking on two leggy beauties. There was a sense of loss, but when she thought of the number of women he had brought here, and that certain lady in England he had not denied—what point was there in prolonging their friendship?

Excited preparations had gone on all day for the engagement party. Miranda had seen and congratulated Mr Heng, and Isabel had been ecstatic. The Empress Hotel was being transformed into Fairyland. Miranda watched the workmen, wishing with all her heart that she could be the innocent now—see these arrangements as part of a lovely love story, not a hard-headed alliance between beauty and riches.

Maidie had asked Miranda to help her dress. It was an honour. They had bought the silver lamé sheath together; now they had to choose the accessories.

They sat in Maidie's room agonising over her earrings. Miranda had put on her own new dress—pale blue and turquoise chiffon—and now forgot her own trimmings while they searched Maidie's jewel box for the longest earrings.

Jake was awash with fringes, white leather and studs. Miranda joined her friends as they went into the Orchid Room in excited anticipation. Mary Ann Moon was resplendent in a sequinned cheongsam, slit as high as was decent. She did have a wonderful figure. Mr Heng looked suitably proud, in scarlet tuxedo and diamanté cummerbund. The three friends took their usual table. The ballroom was crowded to the very doors; then there was a quiet voice suddenly behind Miranda. 'May I beg your spare seat?

It was Jonathan. Jake welcomed him as an old friend, and as he turned to the girls, Miranda couldn't for the life of her be unwelcoming. Jon said hesitantly, 'There aren't many people on their own.'

Jake jumped up and took his hand. 'Where else? Honoured to have you.' He had a way of putting people at ease.

Jon sat down, handsome in white tux and tie. Miranda couldn't help leaning towards him and saying, 'You shouldn't be alone.'

'I know—wrong, isn't it? If I'd known it was a party I'd have hijacked someone to come with me.'

'Don't!' Miranda couldn't stand that sort of banter. She saw his face change as his watched her, understanding her tenderness. In spite of the distance she had managed to keep between them so far, Jonathan reached out and patted her hand—and kept his hand over hers as the happy couple came round to their table. Mary Ann looked radiant.

Jonathan, and then Jake, jumped up, kissed the bride, and shook hands heartily with Heng. The girls expressed their congratulations, and Miranda thought she detected a shade of envy, as Mary Ann looked down at their table and saw Jon's hand over hers beside the full glasses of champagne. Heng said, 'You are among our long-standing friends. I hope—my fiancée and I hope—you enjoy the meal, and have a wonderful time.'

Miranda said quickly, 'I do wish you well. Happiness and joy.' She had had her differences with Mary Ann, but her wishes were sincere.

Maidie said after they moved on, 'Did you see that rock!'

Jake smiled. 'How could you miss it?'

Miranda asked him, 'Are you singing something suitable?'

Jake folded his limbs further down. 'We aren't the stars tonight, honey. There's a heap of big names before us.'

Zendik. . . Miranda tried not to react. She sat back and found that Jonathan was looking at her, concern and care in his eyes. It seemed unreal, both of them here together, celebrating his ex-girl-friend's engagement. . .

And then there was some activity on stage. Some music stands were put in place, a fanfare shattered the polite chatter, then the spotlight swung down spectacularly. It was Zendik, resplendent in white, even to white leather shoes, showing off his dark handsomeness to perfection. He was wildly cheered.

His speech was gentle and to the point. Ladies and gentlemen. . . my privilege. . . loveliest couple in the world tonight. . . Happiest for all their tonights. . . Mary Ann and her Gerald.' There was more applause, and the orchestra began to play softly. The engaged couple took to the floor. After one turn, others began to join in. Jonathan stood up, coaxing Miranda to her feet.

'We ought to do one circle for them to wish them luck.' He was the best-looking man on the floor, in white tuxedo perfectly tailored to his broad shoulders. She was taken smoothly into his arm, and they moved out in time to the music. There was no need to worry about the steps—he led her with confidence, so that they moved as one person. 'Miranda, you should look happy tonight—

it's a celebration,' he reminded her.

'I'm sorry, do I look sad? It must be because this is turning into a bit of a dream. In another week it won't exist.'

'Memories are always like that. The secret is—to make lots more, then you don't regret anything.' Jon swung her round, so that the full skirt of her dress flew out. She couldn't help smiling at the feeling of exhilaration it aroused. 'That's better. Now you're cheering me up too. Now I'm not all alone.'

'You ought to have brought Leonie,' she told him. 'You aren't the kind of man to be alone.'

'No, impossible. I've changed. I can't do that casual affair thing any more.'

'Ah, the lady from England.'

'Yes, little witch who knows everything. You could say the lady from England.'

Miranda tried to keep smiling, but it was difficult, now that he had admitted it honestly. She nestled against his body as they moved in perfect symmetry, and tried to remember the feeling of being with him, knowing that so very soon she would never see him again, never nestle like this, enclosed in the only arms she felt right in. And he bent his head towards her, so that their cheeks were together, warm and sensual. He murmured, 'Here's someone who can make your memories even better.'

'Who's that?'

'The photographer, darling.'

Miranda would have drawn away from Jon as they danced, but he held her close, told her to smile and look happy. The flash of the camera went off two or three times close to them. The mini-skirted Chinese photographer thanked them. 'Your pictures will be in Reception tomorrow morning.' she said, turning to find another couple in the now crowded ballroom. Pleased, Miranda knew she wanted something to take home, something to look at in her secret moments, when she would remember Genting and her surgeon in the clouds.

Then they heard Jake, as the music changed and the tempo slowed. Jon's grasp tightened as they moved slowly, dreamily to Jake's golden voice. Maidie joined in, not perky and lively tonight, but in smooth harmony, as befitted an engagement party. Their song made Miranda's eyes fill with tears. How she would miss her dear friends! Jon stood still in the middle of the floor, mopped at her tears with his perfectly folded white handkerchief, then danced her towards the door, at the far end from the singers. 'Want to go to bed?' he asked 'You look tired.'

She stood, her hand still grasping his arm. 'I don't want to miss anything.'

'It's only Zendik now. He'll do a couple of romantic numbers.'

'I'll go, then. Goodnight.'

'Want me to see you up?'

Miranda shook her head. 'Stay and enjoy yourself. There are a couple of girls looking at you at the moment, so you won't be alone for long.' She smiled up at him. It was hard to let go, but she didn't want to be hurt any more; a romantic evening with someone who was in love with someone else was not Miranda's idea of fun. She walked slowly out of the door, her floating skirt lifting in the slight breeze in the corridor.

She heard the drum roll for Zendik, and paused. She would listen to the beginning, for old times' sake. She heard him talking: 'I'll be singing all the old favourites tonight at the request of the bride.' Cheers and whistles. 'But first, a simple song written by Brad—your pianist here, one of the finest musicians I've ever met. Here it is, maestro.' Miranda heard the piano—it was her piano-player, the man she had listened to in her first weeks at Genting. She went back to the door. It was impossible to see above all the heads, but she knew his playing. He was indeed a musician. Zendik came in after the slow introduction.

The words seemed ordinary enough—he had travelled the world, from desert to frozen ocean, so much became just wandering, but he would never forget Miranda. . . *Miranda*! Brad had written a song about Miranda—and Zendik was singing it, making it immortal. . . She was pretty sure that Zendik didn't know she was here. But he would sing that song—he might record it—it would become known as one of his. And it would be her name—possibly even inspired by her! She felt unbelievably touched and honoured. It was something wonderful, that took away all the unpleasantness that had been caused when she first met the famous singer.

Miranda's last day was misty. She spent it wandering around the hotel, chatting with all the friends she had made, quietly recalling the times they had had. She lunched with Maidie and Jake. It wasn't really a sad occasion, because she had shed all her tears the previous night. They talked of what they were going to do next year, and naturally, they promised that they would always keep in touch. Then Maidie opened a small box she had been keeping on the table. 'Maybe it ain't your style, honey, but wear them when you feel wild, or want to remember us.' They were real diamond earrings, shimmering drops.

They went with her to collect the photographs of the dance. 'Wow, what a picture!' Jake took them from the large board, three pictures of Miranda in Jonathan's arms. She picked them up and stood for a moment lost in thought, hearing the music of last night, remembering their closeness, the way they moved in harmony together. She bit her lip suddenly.

'I don't think I'd better say goodbye,' she decided.

'You'd better not take them all,' advised Maidie. 'Jon might want one for himself.'

Miranda put one back on the board, then looked at her watch. 'I'd better get going. I'll get the next *kabel cerata*.' She hugged Maidie. 'Don't come down. I know the way.' She turned to Jake. 'Will you give this to Jon?' She scribbled on the back of one photograph: 'Yours, Miranda.'

He said quietly, 'Shall I get him to sign one for you?'

'No.' Jonathan was serious about his English lady. It was wrong to push herself on to him, when he was at last showing signs of finding someone to share his life with. Poor man, he had done his Flying Dutchman act for too long already. Let him concentrate on his future, and forget his small visiting Sister he had cared for so tenderly when she lay in his Klinik, delirious. . . He was a good man. She would never forget him.

Miranda walked very slowly along the cool corridor towards the cable station. She had slung her angora sweater round her shoulders, as the mist was chill, as it swirled around outside the hotel like ragged ghosts. But it would get hot fairly soon in the cab to the airport. She carried her one bag like a reluctant schoolgirl, hanging, almost dragging on the ground, as though it were some sort of anchor pulling her back, begging her not to leave Genting.

The car was way down the mountain. She stood leaning on the windowsill looking out at the mist. She would finish her diary on the plane. Just now her memories were too close, her emotions too raw to write down clearly what had happened.

Then the rattling noise increased. The car was on the way up. She turned longingly, to where Jonathan must be. He would understand why she didn't say goodbye; they always understood each other.

She smiled as she recognised the gorgeous conductress with the seductive black eyes who had captivated Bill when they first arrived. The noisy metal gates clanged open and the passengers streamed out, some of the women making straight for the Casino. There would be a twenty-minute wait before the downward trip. There was no hurry; she had plenty of time.

'Miranda!'

She knew who it was, and although she hadn't wanted to say goodbye, she was glad he had thought of her enough to want to come himself. She turned towards him. He was wearing slacks and a V-necked sweater, and his hair was not combed. His eyes were wild—and her heart turned over as she saw something deep and ragged in them, as though he was going through hell. Instinctively she held out her hands to him, and he caught them in his. 'You really cared so little that you didn't come to me?'

Miranda felt choked suddenly. Huskily she said, 'It was because I cared too much. I thought you knew that well enough.'

'That doesn't make sense. Miranda, I vowed that if you didn't come to me it meant you didn't love me, and I'd stay away from you.'

'Jonathan, that's rubbish!' she exclaimed.

'Well, here I am.' Jon wasn't listening to her. 'Here I am with my pride in tatters. You didn't come to me—so I've come to you. Do you know what I'm saying?'

'What the heck has pride got to do with it?' demanded Miranda. 'You went to see a woman in England—your affair of the heart, as you called it. You can hardly expect me to come to you when you're practically engaged!'

The hooter went. Oh no—when there was so much more to say! How could she even start to tell him how she felt in one minute? 'Miranda, if you go away now I'll—disintegrate, you know that?' His eyes were imploring.

Tears running down her cheeks, she said, 'No, you won't. You're tough. Jon—' He caught her to him, and his eyes held hers as they had that very first day, in this very cable car which was getting ready to go down the side of the mountain.

'Can you say to me—goodbye, Jon Smith, I don't love you?'

The conductress was rattling the metal gate. 'No, I can't. Jon—I've saved some money. Oh gosh, I've got to go. I'll come back, Jon—the first chance I get—' She turned and ran for the car. Turning her head, she shouted, 'Don't forget me. I'll come back. . .!'

There were only a few people on the car. Miranda sat alone at the front, mist swirling around her, her eyes blinded with tears. She stared forward, so that no one on the car could see her damp cheeks and woebegone face. Out into the endless mist, the deep chasms that had once frightened her but now gave her comfort because they matched her own anguished, enormous feelings. The car took off, swaying a little as the wind buffeted it. She looked down. Between the scraps of mist she saw the tops of the trees, spangled with dew as though they were decked with diamonds.

She put her hand in her pocket. The photograph was there, and Maidie and Jake's diamonds. She took the picture out, and tried to make out the features of Jonathan Smith, but his face was only a blur. Then a voice came in her ear, 'If you cry on it, it won't last very long.'

She turned to find Jon sitting next to her. 'I couldn't let you go all alone. You looked so little and defenceless.'

'Thank you.' She buried her face in his sweater, was enfolded by a strong arm.

He spoke to the top of her head. 'That extra week I spent in England—I spent it at Alston Magna, sweet.' She looked up, amazed, not caring how dishevelled she looked, as he went on, his nice familiar face calm and smiling as he saw what he wanted to see in her eyes. 'I told your father how much I wanted to marry you, but that I thought you weren't sure. Your mother was sure: she told me what size your finger was.' He took a little packet of tissue paper from his back pocket and unwrapped it very carefully. A solitaire diamond darted blue sparks into the clouds. Jon took Miranda's left hand in his, kissed the fingers before slipping the ring where it ought to be. 'I didn't bring the box, sorry. Too bulky.'

'Mummy told you what size. . .' She was too surprised to think of anything to say.

'And I asked your father for your hand in marriage. What's wrong with that? People do it all the time. *You* were the "lady from England," you little idiot!' He held her hand out in front on them both, making the diamond sparkle. Miranda looked up at him suddenly, and kissed his cheek. There was a sudden burst of applause as the other passengers and the conductress smiled and called congratulations across the little swinging car on the side of the mountain.

'She is the loveliest of them all, Mr Smith.' The cheerful conductress slapped him on the shoulder.

'I know that.' He looked at Miranda. 'You will accept it, won't you, my darling? It doesn't suit me.'

The ring flashed and sparkled like a living, laughing thing. Miranda watched it, knowing why diamonds meant love. 'I can't live with just a diamond ring—I want *you*. But I have to go away and leave you. Can we cancel my flight?' Then she thought of something else. 'What about your "affair of the heart" in Switzerland?

Jon laughed. 'You forget I'm a cardiac man, my sweet. It was a patient I went to see.' Miranda's last doubts vanished.

They stood up ready to get off the car. As they went down the little corridor towards the car park, the conductress shouted, 'God be with you!' Miranda felt tears forming again. She turned to Jon, who was close behind her. 'I'm not going home,' she said firmly.

Jon put his arm round her shoulders and led her towards his green Rover. He slung her bag in first, and then his own. She caught sight of the label. It read 'Smith—London Heathrow!

She sat in the front seat, suddenly feeling very calm and still, as though she had come struggling through a long wind tunnel out into kind warm air. It was all planned! Jon was coming back with her. He must have been making the arrangements ever since he returned from England. She smiled at him as he got in and started the engine. 'You did know I'd say yes?'

'I prayed. I did hope you would have come to me, though.'

'Jonathan, I'll spend the rest of my life making it up to you,' she promised.

'In that case I'll forgive you.'

They swirled down round the mountainside, the Flame of the Forest appearing like an army of maids of honour, decorating the jungle for their triumphal procession. 'What did you think of Daddy?' asked Miranda.

'We got on from the first day. He's keeping a date free in his list of weddings. And I did say that we could probably spend a month or two in Alston Magna, though we'd be very busy in KL the rest of the year, curing the sick and keeping the healthy healthy.'

'Do you think you're taking a bit of a chance with me?' she asked diffidently. 'I've only very recently grown up.'

'I would have taken a chance the very first day I saw you on the cable car. I didn't want to lose that girl with the dark shining eyes and the magic quality of wonder and happiness she spread around her like stardust.'

'That's a lovely thing to say,' she smiled.

Jon smiled back as he drove the last bit of the mountain road, pausing before joining the main city highway past the rambutan stalls. 'You have a very lovely heart,' he told her gently.

'Since you're a cardiac man, I take your word for that.'

'A sense of humour too—what more could I ask?'

'I'll tell you when we're on the plane.'

He couldn't take his eyes from the road just then, as the traffic was thickening all the time. But he smiled in a very pleased sort of way, and reached out and squeezed her hand quite hard.

Mills & Boon

YOU'RE INVITED TO ACCEPT
4 DOCTOR NURSE
ROMANCES
AND A TOTE BAG

🌹 FREE!
Doctor Nurse

Acceptance card

| NO STAMP NEEDED | Post to: Reader Service, FREEPOST, P.O. Box 236, Croydon, Surrey. CR9 9EL |

Please note readers in Southern Africa write to:
Independant Book Services P.T.Y., Postbag X3010, Randburg 2125, S. Africa

YES! Please send me 4 free Doctor Nurse Romances
and my free tote bag – and reserve a Reader Service Subscription for me. If I decide to subscribe I shall receive 6 new Doctor Nurse Romances every other month as soon as they come off the presses for £6.60 together with a FREE newsletter including information on top authors and special offers, exclusively for Reader Service subscribers. There are no postage and packing charges, and I understand I may cancel or suspend my subscription at any time. If I decide not to subscribe I shall write to you within 10 days. Even if I decide not to subscribe the 4 free novels and the tote bag are mine to keep forever. I am over 18 years of age   EP23D

NAME _____

                                                  (CAPITALS PLEASE)

ADDRESS _____

_____

_____ **POSTCODE** _____

The right is reserved to refuse application and change the terms of this offer. You may be mailed with other offers as a result of this application. Offer expires September 30th 1987 and is limited to one per household.
Offer applies in UK and Eire only. Overseas send for details.

Doctor Nurse Romances

Incurable romantics read one before bedtime.

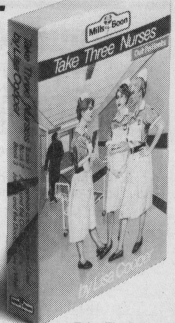

Josephine, Jane and Jacinth were a trio of friends who as students at the Princess Beatrice Hospital in London shared the first years of hard work, laughter and tears.

But now the training is over and the time has come for them to go their separate ways as fully fledged nurses and midwives.

Take Three Nurses is a series of three stories that follow the individual fortunes of each of the three girls on the road to success and romance.

Josephine and a Surgeon of Steel

Jane and the Clinical Doctor

Jacinth and The Doctor Make a Wish

Available from April '87 Price £3.30